DEATH IS A DIRTY TRICK

A terrorist's bomb has blown a private aeroplane out of the sky and killed the famous lawyer J. W. Travers, his daughter, her two young children and the pilot, and set in motion a chain reaction of violence. Only a last-minute change of plan had kept Peter Styles, reporter for *Newsview,* from being a passenger on the plane. Learning that Travers' widow, outraged by the tragedy, threatens to embark on a terror campaign of her own, Peter sets out to identify the perpetrator of the crime, before this basically decent woman gets in too deep for herself.

He finds his investigations blocked at every step. Clearly a powerful adversary is determined to conceal the truth. As Peter's search continues, more tragedies come to light. What secret can be so dangerous that innocent people have to die for it?

Here is a thriller that leads up to a startling and wholly unexpected climax.

ALSO BY JUDSON PHILIPS

Peter Styles Mysteries:

A MURDER ARRANGED
FIVE ROADS TO DEATH
BACKLASH
WALK A CROOKED MILE
THE POWER KILLERS
THE LARKSPUR CONSPIRACY
THE VANISHING SENATOR
ESCAPE A KILLER
NIGHTMARE AT DAWN
HOT SUMMER KILLING
THURSDAY'S FOLLY
THE WINGS OF MADNESS
THE TWISTED PEOPLE
THE BLACK GLASS CITY
THE LAUGHTER TRAP
WHY MURDER?

PART ONE

1

It was only by the purest chance that I wasn't blown into a thousand pieces that summer morning, the bits of my body raining down over the area near Framingham, Massachusetts. I had been scheduled to make the trip from Bartram in J. W. Travers's Beachcraft Baron, a six-place, twin-engine job, along with J. W. himself, Janet Colmer his daughter, and her two kids, Freddie and Elaine, ages ten and eight. Steve Meadows, J. W.'s private pilot, was to fly us.

At the last minute, with the Baron's engines warming up at the end of Bartram Airport's black-topped runway, it was decided that I would not make the trip to Boston. The whys and wherefores are a later part of this account. The point is, I didn't board the Baron and I am alive. All the others are dead; J. W. Travers, Janet Colmer, Freddie and Elaine Colmer, and Steve Meadows, the pilot. About twenty miles from Boston's Logan Airport the Beachcraft Baron, known as "the Cadillac of private planes," blew up. It blew up so violently that no one for a moment considered the possibility of an engine failure. J. W. Travers, famous trial lawyer, had been the target for an assassin's bomb, not unlike the disaster that had overtaken Earl Mountbatten in his yacht off the Irish coast some time back. The others who died, a beautiful young woman of thirty, two vigorous and lovely children, and a former air force pilot, were just unlucky.

I was lucky. I didn't make the trip with the others, but I didn't know how lucky I'd been until hours after the disaster took place. I was driving down a winding Berkshire mountain road in my convertible when I switched on the radio. I wasn't interested in anything particular, just wishing to divert my attention from what I'd been involved with for the last space of time. I found myself pulling to a stop beside the road, stunned by what I heard.

"I have the latest on the disaster in the skies outside Boston a few hours ago," the radio voice said. "We now have a complete list of the victims of what appears to have been an assassin's bomb, detonated by remote control or some other means. The plane, a Beachcraft Baron, was owned by J. W. Travers, famous trial lawyer. With him were Janet Travers Colmer, his daughter, a lady touched by scandal in recent months, her two young children, Peter Styles, well known investigative reporter for *Newsview* magazine, and Stephen Meadows, the pilot."

That's what drew me up at the side of the road. I am Peter Styles.

"The plane took off from Bartram, Massachusetts, where J. W. Travers maintains a summer home," the announcer continued. "The airport there is a small, unsophisticated facility where a dozen or more private planes are hangared, plus a few planes owned by an air-taxi service. Private owners are not required to file any kind of flight plan or passenger list. The list of victims was finally supplied by Mrs. Marilyn Travers, wife—now widow—of the famous lawyer. Her husband, she reports, had business in Boston and decided to take his daughter, his two grandchildren, and Peter Styles, who was a house guest, with him. Styles, according to Mrs. Travers, was involved in researching the story of the scandal that overtook Janet Travers Colmer some months ago. Mrs. Colmer has made headlines over the last ten years as a radical, following the Jane Fonda line of 'economic democracy versus corporate power.' She was accused by the police in a small southern town of being caught in a sexual situation with Jefferson Fry, a well-known black activist. Fry was shot to death by the police police in that raid and, though Mrs. Colmer denied any intimate relationship with the black man, her image as a public figure was badly damaged. J. W. Travers, her lawyer-father, was determined to clear her name and, according to Mrs. Travers, Peter Styles had offered to help."

I shut off the radio and sat there, behind the wheel of my car, fighting off the sensation of shock. Only a few hours ago I had been laughing and playing with those two kids, Freddie and Elaine. Lovely kids. The whole Travers household, despite Janet Colmer's troubles, had been so warm, so alive, so full of good humor and fun. It was almost impossible to take in. They were all suddenly gone, except Marilyn, J. W.'s beautiful, elegant, witty, sophisticated wife. I don't think I ever knew a happier couple in their own relationship. I wondered how Marilyn could survive this, the loss of a husband, a daughter, and two grandchildren in one moment of horror. Survival was almost too much to expect.

I had to get moving. Back in New York my boss at *Newsview*, Frank Devery, and other friends and professional associates would have heard the report that I was dead. Most of them, I hoped, would be glad to hear that I wasn't. And there was Marilyn Travers, so suddenly and desperately alone. She needed help, though God knows what I could do for her.

Some people go through life without ever scraping a fender or slipping on the ice. Others seem to be accident prone, always involved in some minor disaster. There is a third group which faces violence of Greek-tragedy proportions, like the Kennedy family, with two sons assassinated and a third always under a cloud of danger. It would seem that I belong in that third group.

For a while everything seemed to be going my way. I was offered a job on *Newsview* magazine, where I became a sort of man-about-town, involved in the pleasant job of writing witty columns about theaters, nightclubs, and the glamorous people who make them tick. Then one weekend, distressed by my father's state of mind and health, I persuaded him to drive up to Vermont with me to a ski place I knew. I thought fresh air and a change of scene might do him good. It seemed to work a little. Driving down a winding mountain road on our way home two hopped-up kids began to play passing games with us, forcing us closer and closer to the edge of the road— until suddenly we were gone, somersaulting down into a deep ravine. The car burst into flame when we reached the bottom. I was thrown clear, but lay helpless as I heard my father screaming as he burned to death. I passed out and when I came to I was in a local hospital where the doctors had amputated my right leg just below the knee.

I was no longer the gay young "man about town." I had no other interest in the world but to find those two murderous kids and destroy them. I became a kind of crusader against all senseless violence that seemed to be part of our lives in the mid-sixties.

I might not have made it at all except for Frank Devery, the publisher and editor of *Newsview* magazine. Frank is a short, stocky man with sandy brown hair and bright blue inquisitive eyes. He gives the impression of being an almost abrasive, slave-driving kind of man, but those of us who know him and work for him are aware that under that tough outer surface is a warm compassion for people.

He was a rock for me. He got me to stop feeling sorry for myself, kept me busy with absorbing assignments, almost literally held my hand when I needed it. Without him I don't think I would have made it back.

Then Grace came into my life. We married, and it couldn't have been more perfect. I had to go out to the West Coast to follow up on a story I was doing. My research took me into a camp for refugees from Vietnam. Grace felt a deep pity for those homeless, displaced people. I had to jump around to several cities on the Coast and Grace volunteered to help the people at the camp. One night when I was away in San Francisco an army of nameless goons invaded the camp, shooting and killing without rhyme or reason. Grace was among the dead when the bodies were counted.

More urgently than ever I found myself fighting the people who were responsible for senseless violence, and as time went on I became more and more convinced that behind much of it was the greed for wealth and power that motivates the hundreds of multinational corporate giants around the world.

"Keep gunning for them, chum," Devery said to me one day, "and Death will get impatient and run up your number!"

It seemed my number hadn't been up today. Maybe Death wasn't ready for me yet.

I drove down into the town of Bartram and located a public phone booth in the local drug store. I called Frank Devery's private number at *Newsview.*

He answered, his voice sounding harsh, like a stranger's.

"Are you sitting down?" I asked him.

"My God, *Peter!*" he almost shouted.

"I wasn't on the plane, friend," I said.

"Where are you?"

"In Bartram. I only just heard the news myself about fifteen minutes ago."

"But it's been hours!"

"I know. Long story. But first I've got to go to Mrs. Travers. Her whole family's been wiped out, Frank."

"Maxvil's just left here," Frank said. Gregory Maxvil, lieutenant, Manhattan Homicide, is one of my close friends. "God, I hope I can reach him and tell him. He has a theory about what happened."

"Theory?"

"He's talked to explosive experts in his department," Frank said. "They think the bomb must have been attached to the plane there in Bartram, hooked up to the radio. The plane would have to contact Logan Airport when they were twenty miles away—just where it happened. They'd need permission to land and instructions about what runway. The bomb, tuned into the Logan frequency, would explode the minute the pilot tried to make contact. Logan never heard from him. It was that quick and total. What about security at the Bartram airport?"

"I suppose there isn't any, except for a state police

patrol passing by three or four times a night. It's a one-horse operation, Frank."

I heard him draw a deep breath. "It's your story," he said.

"I know, even if you didn't assign me to it. I'm going to get the bastards responsible for this. Count on it."

Big talk. But it was all I cared about at that moment.

"Who do you want me to call?" Frank asked.

"Greg Maxvil, of course. I suggest you pass the word to the local radio stations and the TV people. It will save you a lot of dialing."

He made a chuckling sound. "Would you believe I was working on an elegant obituary of Peter Styles when you called?"

"Save it for me," I said. "People say the nicest things about you when you're dead."

"Peter?"

"Yes."

"I'm so very damn glad, chum," Frank said.

I stood in the booth, juggling a dime. Should I call Marilyn Travers or should I just walk in on her? Would it be harder for her to hear from me and wait, or for me to walk in the door and show myself? Almost certainly she wouldn't answer the phone herself. It might be better not to give a message to one of the servants, or some friend who had rushed to attend her when the news broke. I decided to head straight for the big house back in the hills that J. W. Travers had built years ago and loved so much.

Someone had said that the past is the prologue for the present, and that the present is the prologue for the future. The fairly recent past was the prologue for the slaughter of innocent people in the air over Framingham.

The present would be the prologue for a future that I intended to help shape. Someone was going to have to pay the price for a multiple murder. I wasn't too concerned with finding the man who had placed the bomb and triggered it to go off outside Boston. I wanted the man who had paid to have it done. The trigger man in a murder of this sort is simply an extension of the weapon. The real killer is the man who planned and paid for the job. I thought I knew that man's name. Knowing his name was one thing. Proving his guilt was another.

So there was the fairly recent past. Janet Travers Colmer had made the headlines quite frequently before her flaming death outside Boston that morning. Daughter of J. W. Travers, often referred to as "today's Clarence Darrow," Janet was "rarer meat" to the press than other spirited young girls of her age and time. She was kicked out of college for what was called a "radical demonstration" against the war in Vietnam. J. W. Travers supported his daughter and brought an action against the school, which failed. Those were the days of Richard Nixon and J. Edgar Hoover. Headlines! She eloped to Canada with a young man named Jerome Colmer who was trying to avoid being drafted into the armed services. Headlines! She bore him two children in exile: Freddie and Elaine. J. W. joined his daughter in a long, public fight to gain amnesty for Jerry Colmer. J. W. finally managed a pardon for his son-in-law. Headlines! Charges that "special privilege" had been granted the famous lawyer. Back in this country Janet and Jerry Colmer began campaigning for "Economic Democracy Versus Corporate Power." Headlines once more, since she was J. W. Travers's daughter. She went to a small southern town, Vickers Creek, with Jefferson Fry, the black activist, to protest against a nuclear power plant there operated by

Loring Industries, the big multinational corporation. There Janet met her Waterloo. In a raid on Jefferson Fry's motel room outside Vickers Creek. Janet Travers Colmer, according to the police, was found naked in bed with the black leader. Pictures were taken. Jefferson Fry was shot to death when he tried to escape arrest. Headlines! Scandal!

Janet Colmer denied vehemently that she had indulged in any kind of sexual intimacy with the dead Jefferson Fry. She had been in Fry's room at the motel to discuss a massive demonstration against Loring Industries' nuclear power plant the next day. Men had charged into the room and Janet had found herself, she claimed, with an ether-soaked cloth held over her face. When she came to she was naked, in bed with a dead man, a squad of strong-armed goons jeering at her.

The public in general didn't buy her story. Lee Bullock, the red-neck sheriff of Vickers Creek, claimed she was lying through her teeth. He had caught her "in the act," he said. Fry's motel room had been raided because "we don't intend to let outsiders tell us how to run our town." Fry, according to Bullock, caught in the middle of a sexual moment with Janet, attacked one of the arresting officers and was shot.

The public didn't believe Janet but, worse for her, her husband didn't believe her. Photographs, testimony by the Vickers Creek cops, perhaps something secret between Jerry and his wife, tipped the scales. Jerry Colmer walked out on Janet and his two children.

The one person who believed Janet from the first moment was her father, J. W. Travers. He made it clear, defending her in court against a malicious mischief charge brought by the Vickers Creek prosecutor, that he believed she had been framed and that the framers were the tools of Loring Industries. "Big corporations survive and thrive on dirty tricks," J. W. said in an impassioned plea to the jury. "Those dirty tricks include blackmail, defamation, and any other contrivance designed to turn attention away from their own sinister activities. My daughter was taking aim at Loring Industries, planning a demonstration against a nuclear plant that may endanger all your lives. She was asking for genuine economic democracy against the enormous power of giants like Loring Industries. She was fighting, ladies and gentlemen of the jury, for decent, hard-working, God-fearing, American citizens like you. They framed her. Now you have to choose between setting her free and supporting Loring Industries' world of dirty tricks."

I was there that day in court, listening. I heard the jury's verdict—guilty. She was guilty, they obviously thought, because she had been committing adultery with a black radical. The judge sentenced her to a year in prison, but paroled her into the custody of her father, J. W. Travers.

J. W. Travers took his daughter and her two children to his summer place in Bartram, Massachusetts. Cases he was working on were turned over to his partners and he started a private war. He would prove the truth and expose Loring Industries for what it was.

Having listened to the case in court, I believed in Janet's innocence. I persuaded Devery to turn me loose on the whole rotten mess. I approached J. W. Travers and told him what I was up to. He was delighted. I was invited to Bartram to pool information and ideas with the lawyer. That was why I was there that day, why I had been going to Boston with him where he thought he'd found someone who might talk.

I didn't go to Boston because, just as we were about to

board the Baron at Bartram Airport, J. W. and I saw Jerry Colmer, Janet's estranged husband, driving away from the hangar area. He and Janet had had a small cabin up in the hills and it seemed likely he was headed there. I thought it might be useful to talk to him, which is why I stayed behind, and why I found myself still alive some hours later.

I'm not very different from any other man, I guess, when it comes to dreaming about women. One's tastes change with the passing of the years, though. As a teenager I was fascinated by very young girls with their hair blowing in the wind, their tight little buttocks, their firm little breasts. It didn't matter what they had in their heads, it was only their physical assets that counted. In my mid-twenties, as I was beginning to mature, what women thought about and talked about and how they reacted to life-situations began to matter. Sexual attractiveness stopped being a matter of measurements, became a sum-total of personality, intelligence, and a capacity to share and exchange. I lost interest very early in the game for what are called "one-night stands." I wanted companionship, someone to laugh with and live with.

There were several fairly long-running affairs before Grace came into my life. I regret none of them, remember nothing but pleasant things about them. Those adventures were terminated, I think, because I wasn't ready for the kind of permanence that included marriage and children. Then, at age thirty, came the horror of that Vermont mountain, the sound of my father's screams as he died—a sound that was part of a recurring nightmare for months and months—my own crippling and the certainty that no woman of the kind I went for would want to be involved with a mutilated lover. Then there was Grace, dear, darling Grace. I was a man, and she loved me, admired me, respected me, and it didn't matter if I had two heads. I couldn't wait to marry her, couldn't wait to secure the rest of my life. It would be with her, forever. Then some bigoted kids who hated the yellow-skinned refugees from a war we should never have fought put an end to Grace and to my world with a senseless violence.

The struggle to stay alive after that, to keep moving, keep working, is too painful to think about and only has a slight bearing on what was happening to me in Bartram, Massachusetts, on that warm summer day that had taken on a kind of unreal chill in the sudden climate of mass murder.

But there is a point in mentioning how I felt about women after Grace. I am a man. Nature has made us so that we have an instinct and a desire for coupling with women. After almost a year of unbearable loss I ventured out into the field. Three or four very nice women were willing to give it a try with me. It didn't work. They were kind, they were warm, they were tender—but they weren't Grace. I wasn't ready for sex-for-sex, if I ever could be.

I had just turned forty that summer when I went to Bartram to collaborate with J. W. Travers in an attempt to clear his daughter Janet and point the finger, if possible, at Loring Industries. That was when I met Marilyn Travers.

She was a beautiful woman of fifty-one. She had golden blonde hair. It didn't really matter whether she tinted it or not. It looked like her own. She had high cheekbones, warm blue eyes, and a wide, generous mouth. I remember laughing to myself. Not so long ago—it seemed like not so long ago—a woman of fifty-one would have seemed past middle age, even growing old. Marilyn Travers was ageless. She was, intellectually, a sophisticated, highly-educated, really brilliant woman, with wit and humor and a passion for fair play and justice that she shared with her husband.

J. W. was ten years her senior. She had married him when she was nineteen, bore him a daughter when she was twenty-one. That child had cost them, because, it seems, there could be no more children. But I don't think I had ever seen two people more closely in tune than Marilyn and J. W. I found myself warming to them because they were, I told myself, what Grace and I would have been if we'd been allowed to go on together. You must understand, I never gave a thought to any kind of affair with Marilyn Travers. I had a fondness for her because she was so very good for a very good man. He gave her love and she returned his love and maintained herself as a beautiful, vibrant, desirable object for his love. They were perfection, ideal.

That morning, driving out of Bartram and heading up the mountain for the Travers estate, I was shocked by what I found myself thinking. When I reached the house I would find this striking woman alone, her husband dead, her child dead, her grandchildren dead. All the love in her life had been wiped out in one explosive moment. There were no words that could be spoken to her that would do any good. The only possible solace might come from taking her in my arms, holding her close, letting her feel the sympathy and love I had for her.

I stepped down hard on the gas. I was, for God sake, thinking of myself and not Marilyn!

J. W. Travers had built himself a colonial-type mansion on the side of a hill, looking out over a valley where the town lay, and on beyond to the rising Berkshires. It was a warm house, like the people who lived in it—had lived in it. The furniture was a variety of antique and modern, but comfortable, with no suggestion of an interior decorator's finger in the pie. I think Marilyn had furnished it with things she liked, including paintings, some of which were her own, without any relationship to a scheme or plan. Sometimes it seemed cluttered with the grandchildren's toys, with golf clubs, with books and papers scattered around. J. W. collected guns, and there was a room for them. Moments later everything would be in place. A competent couple, Charles and Helen Shay, kept the wheels turning at Travers Hill. You felt welcome when you walked in the front door, by the house itself and whoever might appear.

The one hostile note about the place were the huge iron gates that guarded the entrance to the grounds. They could be operated, electrically, from the house. If J. W. Travers wanted to shut out the world, he could, and sometimes did.

That dreadful morning the gates were closed. There were a dozen cops and a score of people clustered around outside. With them was a young man named Al Bostick, a blond, hard-faced guy who sometimes acted as a bodyguard for J. W., sometimes as chauffeur, sometimes just as a friend. J. W. had trusted and counted on him. His job now was to protect Marilyn from the local press and reporters from far away who had come on the run. There had been hours since the explosion in which they could begin to collect.

Al Bostick's young face looked as though it had suddenly been carved in marble. He faced me as I got out of my car and I approached him.

"I'm sorry, but Mrs. Travers is not seeing anyone," he said. Then his jaw dropped open in an almost comical double-take. "*Mr. Styles!*"

I reached out and put my hand on his shoulder. "Take it easy, Al," I said.

"You escaped it!" he said.

"I wasn't on it," I said.

"But we thought—"

"I wasn't on it, Al, or I wouldn't be here. Who is with Mrs. Travers?"

"Mr. Tyler. He just got here a few minutes ago. Charles and Helen. I don't understand—?"

Sam Tyler was J. W.'s law partner. Marilyn had someone with her. I was suddenly surrounded by others waiting outside the gate. Al Bostick hadn't been quiet about identifying me.

"You are Peter Styles?" a young man asked me.

"Yes."

"We were told you were on the plane! It's been on the radio, on television."

"Obviously I wasn't," I said. I drew Al Bostick aside. "I don't want Mrs. Travers to be too shocked, Al. Will you go up to the house and tell Mr. Tyler I'm here? He'll break the news to her."

Sam Tyler had been J. W.'s close friend since their law school days. He was just the right person to be with Marilyn, I thought. Perhaps I should simply go away until, hearing the news, she sent for me. I didn't go.

The reporters crowded around me. What had happened? Where had I been? I explained, without specifics, that at the last minute I'd decided there was someone in the area I wanted to interview. I hadn't heard about the disaster until a half an hour ago, didn't know that I was listed among the dead. Radio and TV would be correcting the mistake presently. What theories did I have? Could I guess who was responsible?

"So far I don't know any more about it than you do," I said. I didn't tell them that I thought I could name a name without having a shred of proof. Without proof the man I had in mind would have time to build a Chinese wall around himself, from behind which he could take direct aim at me. If Death was impatient, as Frank Devery had suggested, I could make it easy for him if I took a wrong turn.

Al Bostick beckoned to me from the far side of the gate. "Mr. Tyler says for you to come in," he said.

"Does Mrs. Travers know?"

"He's telling her, I think," Al said.

2

As I crossed the lawn toward the house there was something hostile and different about the feel of the place. On a warm, sunny afternoon the kids, Freddie and Elaine, were usually screaming at each other and splashing around in the swimming pool in the back of the house, probably with friends. Not anymore. J. W. had built a special putting green off the terrace on the east side of the house. He normally spent the late afternoons there, sharpening his skills with an old goosenecked putter. His guests were his victims. He loved to play for high stakes and he knew every blade of grass on that green. Come to think of it, his life had been based on high stakes, down to the last moment he'd drawn breath. He had been out to bring down the top man or men in Loring Industries, perhaps the most powerful corporate entity in the world, who had damaged his beloved daughter.

There was a dog, a beautiful tan boxer with white markings at his throat and with huge white feet. His name was Digger. He and I had become friends. Normally he would come dashing across the lawn to greet me.

Not today. Death had turned the whole place cold and forbidding.

Just before I reached the front door it opened and Charles Shay, the houseman, waited for me. He is a big man with, what I think of as, a sweet face. He looked ravaged.

"I couldn't believe it when Al told us, Mr. Styles," he said. "If you got away, is it possible—?"

"I wasn't on the plane, Charles. I didn't go at the last moment."

"God was with you."

"I guess. How is she taking it, Charles?"

Tears rolled up into Charles's dark, limpid eyes. "Her whole world," he said. "My whole world! Helen and I been working for them for the last twenty-five years. Mr. John, he treated us like we were his own people, his own family." Charles was the only person I ever heard use J. W.'s first name. He wiped the tears from his face with the sleeve of his white house coat. "She's froze up, not human," he said.

"Does she know about me?"

"Mr. Tyler told her. They're in Mr. John's study, expecting you."

The study was a small library, lined with calf-bound law books. There was a big, flat-topped desk, cluttered with papers and notebooks. There were leather armchairs and a leather-covered couch. On the north side of the room was a picture window looking out toward the hills. Marilyn Travers was standing there, her back to me as I came in. Sam Tyler sat in one of the leather chairs, hands covering his face. He lowered them as I came in. He is a dark, handsome man, sixty-one or two, grey at the temples. The typical "man of distinction." Lines at the corners of his eyes and mouth were deepened by grief. J. W. had been his lifelong friend and partner.

"Styles," he said, in a low voice. I guess he didn't trust himself to say anything more.

I stood just inside the door, waiting for Marilyn to recognize my presence. Tyler turned to look at her, also waiting. She spoke at last, not facing me. Her voice was hard, bitter, not a voice I'd ever heard before.

"I don't suppose it would surprise you to know, Peter, that I would give anything on earth if it was J. W. who'd come back and not you."

"I didn't come back," I said quietly. "I never went."

She turned to me, and this warm, beautiful woman had been transformed into a pillar of ice. I might have passed her on the street without recognizing her. She was cold, cold, cold. Her eyes were narrowed, partly hiding an almost frighteningly fierce anger. The normally smiling and generous mouth was a thin, tight slit.

"How did that happen?" she asked me.

"We were just about to board the plane at the airport here when Janet saw her husband driving away from the hangar area," I said.

"Jerry? Jerry Colmer?"

"Yes. I understand he and Janet had a small plane before they split up. J. W. bought it for them, I suppose."

"Who else?" Marilyn said. "He bought them most of what they had. He financed their crazy trips and demonstrations. He made it possible for her to get into the trouble she was in. He loved her too damned much!"

"So did you," Sam Tyler said, in a low voice.

"I'm not sure I remember what you're talking about. Love?"

She was over the edge, I thought.

"What did seeing Jerry have to do with your not taking the trip to Boston?" Marilyn asked.

I told her that Janet had been pretty shaken up at seeing her husband. They used to fly their plane to Bartram from New York for weekends in their cottage across the valley.

"The cottage J. W. built them," Marilyn said.

"Janet thought he might be going there," I said. "She thought—she hoped, I think—he might be going to try to see her. If Colmer might be going to have a change of heart about Janet, was thinking of some sort of reconciliation, she wanted to go to him. J. W. needed her in Boston. He suggested that I might follow Colmer to the cottage, let him know where Janet was and when she'd be back—"

"Like never," Marilyn said in that harsh, cold voice.

"J. W. thought that, in view of what we'd begun to believe, I might be able to persuade Colmer that Janet had always told him the exact truth about Vickers Creek," I said. "Janet begged me to go, so I went."

"And how is dear, kind, trusting Jerry?" Marilyn asked.

"I spent four hours with him," I said. "I think I made him a believer."

"My gallant son-in-law has always been too late for anything that mattered," Marilyn said. Bitter, so damned bitter. "How did he take the news?"

"He didn't," I said. "He didn't have it. While I was with him we didn't listen to radio or television. I didn't know myself till I was halfway back to town; on my car radio. A good four hours after the rest of the world knew. He may not know now."

Tyler pulled himself up out of his chair. "I'll phone him," he said.

"There's no phone in the cottage," Marilyn said. "It

doesn't matter when he finds out. He won't be any use to me. He hasn't got the guts!"

"Guts for what?" I asked.

The ice-blue eyes fastened on me. "You don't suppose I'm going to let Stanley Capra get away with this, do you?"

She had mentioned the name that had been in the back of my mind for days, long before the tragedy. Stanley Capra, chairman of the board of Loring Industries, was the man I thought might have framed Janet in Vickers Creek and planned and paid for the elimination of J. W. Travers and the others today.

"We're a long way from being able to prove Capra is involved," I said.

Marilyn brought a clenched fist down hard on the back of the leather couch. "Do you think I give a damn about proof, Peter? I'm going to kill the sonofabitch!"

Tyler looked at me and gave me a helpless little shrug of his elegant shoulders. I guessed he'd tried to talk her out of that nonsense before I got there, obviously without any luck.

I've just called Marilyn's outburst "nonsense," but, brother, did I understand how she felt and did I sympathize with it! I could wake from a deep sleep and still hear my father's screams as he was roasted alive. I could still remember the violent rage that shook me when, in a hospital bed, I reached down and found that a part of my right leg was no longer there. I didn't want to do anything but kill in those moments. I think if I'd ever been able to find those two vicious young hoodlums who forced my car off the road, killed my father, and left me mutilated, I wouldn't have hesitated for a minute, regardless of the eventual cost to me. I didn't kill anybody then because I never was able to locate and identify those two goons. Looking down at a slab in a California morgue at what was left of my wife, Grace, I would have killed in a flash if I could have fingered her murderers. I knew exactly how Marilyn was feeling.

There was an extra dimension in Marilyn's situation. I never knew who wrecked my car, killed my father, cost me a part of a leg. I could never put a name or a face to anyone. I could never put a name to the persons who shot away Grace's lovely face with a machine pistol. Marilyn had a name and a face. Stanley Capra is a public figure, head of a huge conglomerate, socially prominent. Even if you didn't know him, you'd probably recognize him if you passed him on the street. He's appeared before congressional committees, at charity drives, as a supporter of leading political figures—all on television. He's as well known as a movie star. Marilyn had a totally recognizable target for her fury. If—if he was guilty!

I don't think in all his life with Marilyn, thirty-two years, that J. W. Travers ever had a secret from her. He talked over his cases with her. He was a man—how shall I say it?—who liked to think vocally. It was as if ideas developed better for him when he talked about them to someone. Marilyn was always there when he needed to talk. Since I'd been involved with J. W., Marilyn had often been present during our conversations about the Vickers Creek business and she had contributed to them.

There was no doubt in our three minds that Janet Colmer had been framed in Vickers Creek. She had a name, she was J. W.'s daughter. Fronting a demonstration against Loring Industries' nuclear power plant in Vickers Creek was attracting attention. They needed to discredit her, silence her. Who knows, perhaps Loring

Industries stole a leaf from the FBI's book. We have been led to believe that the late Jean Seberg, movie star, was a target for defamation by J. Edgar Hoover. It was carefully rumored that a baby she was carrying had been fathered by a black man, a member of the Black Panthers. Miss Seberg had publicly supported the black organization. Miss Seberg's husband claimed the child was his, that it was white. Her effectiveness, however, as a supporter of radical causes was brought to an end. The defamers won the ball game. The unhappy Miss Seberg eventually committed suicide.

Personally, I concede there may be many reasons to object to or regret an affair between a married woman and a man not her husband. To me, however, the color of the man's skin is of no importance at all. He could be black, blue, yellow, green, or pink! A man is a man is a man. But despite all the social, educational, and political advances made in the last twenty-five years, there is still a deep prejudice against a white woman sleeping with a black man, particularly in a southern town like Vickers Creek. Janet's framers knew what they were up to. Jefferson Fry, the black man, a real danger to Loring Industries, could be shot dead without any outcry or any legal charges against the man or men who shot him. There would be no questions asked because, they said, he'd been found in bed with a white woman.

Stanley Capra didn't raid that motel room, didn't shoot Jefferson Fry, didn't hold an ether-soaked cloth over Janet's face and then strip her naked in front of a gang of salivating creeps. But it was J. W.'s theory, and mine, and, God help us, Marilyn's, that none of it could have happened without Stanley Capra's approval. How to prove that was something else again.

Today J. W. and Janet, and three others, had died

violently. Why? Because J. W. was working to get that proof, no secret to Capra and the rest of the Loring Industries hierarchy. They evidently thought J. W. was getting too close. That was something I was left to prove.

Marilyn, in today's horror climate, didn't care about proof, only punishment. You walk on eggs with someone in Marilyn's state of mind.

"Knowing what you do about me, Marilyn, you know how deeply I sympathize with what you're feeling. I know all about the impulse to square accounts," I said to her.

"Then help me!" she said.

"Help you do what?"

"I'm not going to shoot Stanley Capra from behind a tree while he's walking his dog in the park," Marilyn said. "I mean to confront him, let him know why he's going to die, and give him a moment of terror I'll enjoy for the rest of my life!" A corner of her mouth twitched. "Do you suppose J. W. and the others had such a moment before—before it happened?"

"No. They never knew what hit them."

"Stanley Capra is going to know before he gets hit," she said. "Will you help me, Peter?"

"I'll help you get proof," I said.

"It's been months and there's no proof about Vickers Creek," she said. "More months and there may be no proof about today. I don't plan to wait months and months for proof. Have you ever heard of anyone in Stanley Capra's position going to jail for a crime he approved but didn't commit?"

I didn't answer because the only answer I had would support her position.

"J. W. has a man down in Vickers Creek," Sam Tyler said, from the depths of his armchair. "A first-rate private investigator. Someday, sooner or later, someone down there will be persuaded to talk. Someone may be willing to take money to talk."

"Sooner or later is too late!" Marilyn said.

"This thing today begins here in Bartram," I said. "Someone had to plant a bomb on J. W.'s plane during the night." I explained Maxvil's theory about the bomb being set to go off when the pilot tried to contact Logan Airport. "The wheels have only just started to turn here, Marilyn. We could get lucky for a change."

"I'm not interested in getting lucky," Marilyn said. "All I care about is making certain I nail Stanley Capra to the nearest barn door!"

She turned and walked quickly, with a kind of frightening determination, out of the room.

"I suppose this will pass," Sam Tyler said after a moment.

"It has never really passed for me," I said. "If I suddenly found myself facing the people who killed my wife I can't promise you I'd wait for evidence that would stand up in a court case."

"It's a Christ-awful business," Tyler said. "What about Jerry Colmer? If he doesn't know what's happened shouldn't someone be telling him? His wife and his children—"

"He may have turned on his radio by now."

"And what does he do? Does he come here? I suspect he knows how Marilyn feels about him. She hates his guts for turning his back on Janet and the kids."

"They have a grief to share. That may square things between them," I said, and didn't believe a word of it. Marilyn Travers wasn't going to share her grief with anyone; not her husband's partner, not her daughter's husband. You don't share a plan to commit a murder with anyone. She was going to have to share it with me, if I had to break her arm. Stopping her was the last thing I could do for J. W. Travers, a man I'd admired, who would want her safe and his killer dealt with in a legal fashion. Next to Marilyn I suspect the law, the justice system, had mattered most to J. W.

I remembered talking to him about Janet's problems. "One thing I can do," I'd said, "is get Lee Bullock, that Vickers Creek sheriff, in a back alley and beat the truth out of him."

He gave me that lazy, warm smile of his. "Evidence is what we're after, Peter, not fun."

I remember that because he was right. There are times in a man's life when he thinks of violence as fun. He wants it so badly he can taste it. I had felt that way twice. By luck, or mismanagement, or whatever, I was cheated out of it. I never caught up with the people I wanted so desperately to hurt. If I'd had it my way at the time, I would probably be serving out a life sentence in jail somewhere, or sweating it out on some prison's death row.

Marilyn had to be stopped.

I am a good reporter, mostly self-trained but with considerable help from Frank Devery. "The first thing a good investigative reporter has to ask himself," Devery often said, "is 'Where is the action?' " I am not a police reporter who covers the holdup of a liquor store or a branch bank. Police are trained to investigate such details as fingerprints, ballistics reports that may identify a gun, the questioning of possible witnesses. The kind of story I'm usually after lies behind the crime, the disaster, the scandal. The law arrests the people who break into offices and bugged telephones in the Watergate scandal. Woodward and Bernstein, the reporters who broke the story, asked themselves the big question—"Where *is* the action?"—and dug for it and found the answer. In Vickers Creek the action wasn't in the motel room where a bribed sheriff and his men framed a woman and murdered a man. The police and the courts had cleared them of any wrongdoing. The action that mattered to me and had mattered to J. W. lay somewhere else, where the scheme had been dreamed up, authorized, set in motion.

Today's mass murder of five people presented the same problem. Someone had planted a bomb during the night on J. W. Travers's Beachcraft Baron. The police might find fingerprints, a witness, some other evidence. They might even arrest an explosives genius who was responsible. But unless that genius talked, and unless he had more to talk about than the name of someone who had paid him to do the job, we still wouldn't know where the action was. Because he would never have been within miles of Stanley Capra or anyone else high up in the power structure of Loring Industries. This kind of thing was too cleverly and carefully planned to leave any kind of trail to where the real action was. Where was I to begin? Looking into the future, it seemed to me the proof, which I'd told Marilyn I meant to find, that I'd told Devery I meant to find, was an obscured goal. There would almost certainly be no bugged telephones, no secret tapes of conversations carelessly kept. Capra was far too clever to leave any loose ends like that. He could pay so generously for silence that it would be a miracle if anyone could be persuaded to talk.

Sam Tyler had set out to find Jerry Colmer and give him the news if he still hadn't heard it. I had walked out onto the lawn, hoping the sunshine might make me feel warm again. Suddenly, across the grass, I saw Digger, the boxer dog, standing like a statue, staring at me. It was as if he was waiting for me to tell him that it was all right for him to come.

"Hey, boy!" I called out to him.

He came bounding toward me. If I ever own a boxer I'll think of calling him "Down Boy." His big white paws were on my shoulders, almost knocking me flat. A great, slavering tongue took a swipe at my cheek. I said it. "Down, boy!"

He was really a very well-behaved beast. He sat, looking up at me. I knelt down beside him, stroking him, talking nonsense to him which he seemed to understand. He needed love, as did everyone in that Godforsaken place that afternoon. J. W., his master, his life, was gone forever, and he seemed to know it.

"You're a nice man, Peter," a voice said from behind me.

I turned to see Elizabeth Ryan. In all the tension I had forgotten that she was here at Travers Hill. She is a nice-looking girl in her early thirties. She has been J. W.'s personal secretary for a number of years. She had come up from New York the night before and only missed making the trip with J. W. to Boston because, counting me, the Beachcroft Baron was going to be full. She has dark hair, a kind of snub-nosed, good-humored face, slim hips, and rather sensational breasts. I wonder if women dislike the fact that men, in describing them, always mention hips and breasts? Or does it flatter them? She was wearing dark sunglasses. I suspected she must have been crying. Like most secretaries who work closely with a man, I think Beth Ryan had been fonder of J. W. than she would have been willing to admit.

"He seems to know," Beth said, reaching down to the dog.

"Is it an old wives tale, dogs howling when something happens to their masters, miles away?"

"J. W. loved him."

"And you. Maybe all of us who've lost him."

"Oh my God, Peter," she said, and she was suddenly in my arms, weeping.

She is a good, tough girl, though. She had it under control in a moment. She stepped away. "Tears don't do any good," she said.

"Unless they make you feel better."

"The children!" she said. "They were just beginning to enjoy life." The dark glasses were turned away from me. "Do you think there was time for them to be frightened? To suffer?"

"No," I said. "Meadows turned on the radio and that was that."

"How did you happen not to go?" Beth asked me.

I told her. The black glasses turned my way again.

"What was Jerry doing here?"

"A mixed-up man, a long story," I said.

I had never met Jerome Colmer before the morning of that day, a day that, somehow, seemed to involve forever. Those of us who were Boston-bound had left Travers Hill for the Bartram airstrip a little after eight in the morning in my car—J. W., Janet Colmer, and the two kids. My car had been chosen since I would be leaving it behind anyway. That would make the two Travers cars available for Marilyn and for the Shays to go shopping. The kids, Freddie and Elaine, were excited about the trip, not because of the flight or the plane. Flying was old stuff to them. They had never been to Boston—and, God help them, they were never going to see it.

Meadows, the pilot, already had the Baron out on the runway, warming up the twin engines, when we pulled onto the field. The kids ran to say hello to Meadows, an old friend. I heard Janet cry out, and saw her tugging at J. W.'s arm, pointing toward the parking lot we'd just left. A tall, blond man was driving off in an old Volkswagen convertible, a top-down bug. I realized from what she was saying to J. W. that the blond was her estranged husband.

Most of what I knew about Jerry Colmer came from biased sources. J. W. had been his friend and his legal counsel in the draft-evasion business. I don't know how well J. W. liked his son-in-law, but he had fought for him, helped him, and contributed to his family's living in luxurious style. Janet loved him and that was enough for J. W. Then came Vickers Creek and Jerry ran out on his wife and kids. Whatever J. W. had felt for him was transformed into a cold fury.

I don't think Marilyn had ever had much use for Jerry. Basically, I don't think she went in for demonstrations against the status quo. She didn't sympathize with Jerry's evading the draft. I think she thought he was responsible for Janet's radical views. I had the feeling it was the other way around, but no matter. The children, when they arrived on the scene, broke down some of Marilyn's hostility. They were her grandchildren, her flesh and blood, Janet's whom she loved—perhaps too much, as Sam Tyler had said a while back. But when Jerry walked out on Janet after Vickers Creek, any putting up with him by Marilyn turned into the same anger and outrage that J. W. felt.

The children, Freddie and Elaine, had given me another picture of their father. They loved him. They missed him. They admired him. Freddie had an old college yearbook of Jerry's which he read like a Bible. Jerry had been an All-Ivy League halfback; there were pictures of his championship team. Jerry sat in the center of one picture, holding a football. He had been the team's captain as well as its star. Freddie looked blank when Vickers Creek was mentioned. He wanted to believe in his mother, but he knew that J. W., his much-loved grandfather, would defend her, guilty or innocent. He found it hard to believe, however, that his father would desert them if "mum" was innocent. Mixed up.

Janet herself knew she was innocent. She professed to understand why Jerry doubted her; so much evidence, the court verdict in spite of J. W.'s skillful defense. She still loved Jerry, and someday she and J. W. would prove the truth and Jerry would come back.

And there he had been this morning, just driving away from Bartram Airport. One look at Janet and I knew how deeply hooked she was. Jerry was her man, no matter how he had treated her, no matter that he didn't believe her.

"You suppose he's going to the cottage, Dad?" she'd asked J. W.

"Perhaps he's just returning the plane and heading back to the city," J. W. said.

"I don't think so. I want to go to him, Dad. I've got to!"

"We're due in Boston in an hour," J. W. said.

J. W. had located a young professor at Harvard who had grown up in Vickers Creek. His name was Virgil Hardesty. He had contacted J. W. to express an interest in Janet's case. He knew Vickers Creek inside-out. He knew Lee Bullock, the sheriff who'd staged the raid on the motel and framed Janet—if we were right. Hardesty thought he might give J. W. some leads, and it was important for Janet to be there to provide details, to describe some of the men in the raiding party. I wanted to hear what Hardesty had to say about Vickers Creek, a small town obviously controlled by Loring Industries. But I could wait; I could get it from J. W. later. It was essential that Janet talk to Hardesty.

I offered to go to the cottage and, if necessary, sit on Jerry Colmer's head till Janet got back. It was that decision, gratefully accepted by Janet, that saved my life.

Following directions Janet gave me, I caught up with Colmer at the cottage back in the wooded mountainside not ten minutes after he'd arrived there himself.

Introductions. He knew who I was. I'd done a piece for *Newsview* on Janet's trial at Vickers Creek. Naturally he'd read everything written about it. He'd seen his wife and children and J. W. and me arrive at the airport just as he was driving out.

"I thought I'd missed the boat," he told me.

Janet's college-football hero had gone to seed, I thought. He was a little puffy around uneasy grey eyes, and he'd developed a nice little pot for himself. I had the feeling he wouldn't have the wind to run the length of a football field. He was anything but the kind of lean, hard-driving radical I'd expected.

"You came here to see Janet?" I asked him.

"In a way. The Cub I flew up here in is hers. J. W. gave it to her—to us. She doesn't fly it herself, but it belongs to her. I had to return it to her, and I have some things here in the cottage I need. But I meant to try to see her."

"Changed your mind about her?" I asked.

We were sitting in the morning sunshine on a small stone terrace outside the cottage. He was, I thought, a man who had been hurt, wounded. He didn't stand pain well.

"Maybe I've changed my mind about myself," he said. He smoked a cigarette as though it was oxygen he needed. "I didn't think I could live with a lie. I find it doesn't matter. I love Janet. And, oh God, I love the kids."

"They talk about you all the time," I said.

"They do?"

"They do. What is the lie you can't live with, Jerry?"

He looked away as though he hoped to see something helpful in the distance. "I don't care what she says in public," he said. "I don't care what J. W. says in court. But when you live with someone, share your life with someone, you have to tell the truth."

"The truth about what?"

He tossed his cigarette away and lit another one. I saw that his hands weren't too steady. "I can forgive Janet for having an affair with Jefferson Fry," he said. "He was a very alive, vital guy, full of animal magnetism."

"But black," I said.

Colmer looked at me. "Can you believe that matters only a very little? I suppose there are the remnants of some kind of childhood prejudice in me. I've learned over the years—and, for God sake, Janet has helped me to learn it—that a good man is a good man, no matter what the color of his skin, or his race, or his religion. What I haven't learned, I guess, is not to be jealous or possessive about a woman I love. You see, in the very beginning, before Janet and I were married, we talked a lot about sex—sex with other people. We agreed that neither one of us should ask for a commitment from the other. If I felt like having another girl I was free to; if Janet felt like having another man there were no rules against it."

"How very modern," I said.

"Only neither of us chose to have anyone else in those days," Colmer said. "We were free, but nothing in that freedom attracted us. Then Janet got pregnant, and we decided on marriage. The child, who turned out to be

Freddie, was entitled to a legalized situation. We were still free, we told ourselves, but it didn't really matter because we didn't want anyone else. We had each other and eventually our two kids."

"I'm following you very slowly," I said.

"There was the fight to get me out of Canada, and become a free man back here," Colmer said. "Thanks to J. W. we won that fight. Janet and I were all steamed up by what we saw going on in this country: the power in the hands of big money, big business, big corporations. We involved ourselves with what you would call radical groups. We were particularly concerned with the nuclear energy thing. Did you know that there was a nuclear accident in Russia which laid waste a thousand square acres of the countryside, killed thousands of people, and made that part of the countryside uninhabitable for the next hundred years, maybe forever?"

"I've heard the story," I said. "I don't know whether it's true."

"So it might have happened in Harrisburg, Pennsylvania—at Three-mile Island," he said. "It could happen tomorrow in Chicago, or at Vickers Creek. Well, fighting that whole nuclear power situation, we fell in with Jefferson Fry and his black activists. They were fighters, made me almost ashamed of how little we were doing, risking for the cause. Janet was fascinated with them. Fry, I believe, was really dangerous to people like Loring Industries. Fry and his people bored away at them at their very foundations, like termites. He made what we were trying to do seem exciting." Colmer hesitated. "One night Janet came home from a meeting somewhere and told me that Jeff Fry had asked her to go to bed with him. I—I felt threatened. She was free. That was our agreement. 'Do you want to?' I asked her. She smiled at me. 'It might be fun,' she said. We had talked that way before, about women who showed an interest in me, men who had an eye for Janet. It didn't mean we meant to do anything about it. But this time—this time I thought she really was interested. I wasn't as willing, as I always thought I would be, to let her take advantage of our 'freedom agreement.' I watched them together and I saw he was hot for her. And then she went to Vickers Creek for the demonstration there. I stayed in New York with the kids." He paused, and I saw that his fists were clenched in his lap. "So it happened. They were caught together."

"You don't believe her story—the ether-soaked cloth, the rest of it?"

"Of course I don't," he said. "I know why she told it that way. I know why J. W. tried to make a jury believe it. It wasn't just to save her reputation. It was the cause. But, God damn it, I deserved the truth!"

"And you don't think you got it?"

"No. She denied it, like a stuck record. I tried to tell myself it was because of the kids. They were old enough to read the papers, listen to radio, watch TV. But she could have been honest with me. If she couldn't admit the truth to me, I couldn't go on living with her."

"But now?"

"Now, if she'll have me back, I don't give a damn. I love her. If she wants that lie between us I can live with it."

I stood up. I wasn't enjoying myself. "It can't matter to you, but I believe she told you the truth," I said. "I know she wants you back. They're due to return from Boston before dark tonight. No landing lights at Bartram Airport. Shall I tell her you'll be here at the cottage if she wants to come to you?"

"You think she would?"

"I know she will," I said.

I didn't dream, of course, that she wouldn't, couldn't, not ever. While we were talking she was being blown into pieces over Framingham. Jerry and I were not faithful old dogs who sensed disaster at a distance.

I felt free to tell Beth Ryan the whole of that story. She was in on all the notes and the transcripts of the Vickers Creek trial. She had transcribed bushels of tapes J. W. had made of his own thinking on Loring Industries, his conversations with me, with Marilyn, with dozens of experts on corporate law, corporate practices. She had drawn up an elaborate dossier on Stanley Capra, from the day of his birth, his family, his education, his climb to power in Loring Industries, down to what he had for lunch in his office yesterday to where he and his socially-minded, elegant wife, Nancy, were dining out. With J. W. gone, Beth Ryan was going to be indispensable to any story I might write, to the police investigating a mass murder. She was the guardian, the protector, of all the information J. W. had gathered about Vickers Creek, about Loring Industries, about Stanley Capra.

"Poor devil," Beth said. "Jerry's never going to know for certain the truth about Janet, is he?"

"He'll be convinced in time of one thing or the other," I said.

"Where does all this leave you, Peter?" she asked.

"Over a barrel for the moment," I said. "I should be down at Bartram Airport picking up on what, if anything, the cops have found there. I should be heading for Framingham, where there may be something helpful. And I should stay here until someone talks some sense into Marilyn."

"You don't believe she's serious, do you?"

"Of course she's serious. I've been there myself. I know."

"Oh my God, Peter!"

She knew my story, of course. Everyone who can read a newspaper, or listen to radio, or watch TV knows my story. I had been forced to grieve in public, and Marilyn and all of J. W.'s people were in the same boat. The whole country would be fascinated by an extraordinary violence. We have a rapacious appetite for violence.

"Marilyn will live with revenge, dream it, eat it, sleep it," I said. "It won't go away from her for one minute of any day of her life. Unless—"

"Unless what, Peter?"

"Unless someone gets to the truth and nails Capra before she can. In my case, Beth, I never knew who I was looking for, never found out. In her case she thinks she knows—and I think she's right."

"We—we'll just have to surround her," Beth said.

"Possible for a few days," I said. "There'll be funerals—for five people. After that nothing, no one, is going to be able to stop Marilyn from going after what she wants."

"She has to be stopped!"

"So pray for a miracle," I said.

"What kind of a miracle?"

"That in all the material you have, that at Bartram Airport, that in the wreckage of the plane outside Framingham, there is something that will destroy Stanley Capra before Marilyn gets to him."

3

Three days, four days, before the eulogies would be spoken. There would be no bodies to bury. Then revenge and murder would be the name of the game. To forestall it with facts or evidence seemed almost laughably impossible. Capra was protected like a king or a prime minister or a president. Marilyn wasn't the only person in the world who wished him dead. Getting past his guards and secret protectors was a very long-odds chance. Flourish a gun at him and you'd probably be dead before you ever had a chance to aim it. It wasn't Capra who was in mortal danger. It was anyone else, like Marilyn, out to get him. The one way to get Capra was with legal evidence that couldn't be erased by another violence. In three or four days? J. W. Travers, one of the most brilliant legal minds of the time, had spent months looking for such evidence and came up empty. What chance did I have to swing it overnight? None at all if I just sat on my behind here in Bartram brooding about it.

I made a couple of calls from J. W.'s study. One was to Frank Devery in New York. He had no more concrete information than when I'd first talked to him. The FBI had no doubt that the mass tragedy outside Boston was planned assassination. We had a reporter in Boston and he was on the scene, but had come up with nothing yet.

"I'm coming to town after a stop at the airport here," I told Frank. "Probably three or four hours if I spend some time there. I want to locate Stanley Capra. Where is he? New York? Europe? I want to find him, Frank." I told him about Marilyn.

"You can count on Capra's having been quite visible at the critical times," Frank said. "Remember the days of violence on the waterfront? The key bosses were always at their country places on the Jersey coast surrounded by friends when someone got knocked off."

"Try to find out for me where he was and is," I said.

"You can't help the lady unless you can keep her occupied some other way," Frank said.

"Do what I ask, will you, chum?"

"Sure," he said.

"Did you contact Greg Maxvil? Does he know I'm still alive and kicking?"

"He knows."

"I'll call him when I get to town. I may need his help."

"You're going to need help, plenty of it," Frank said.

My second call was to Joe Steiger, a private eye who has done work for *Newsview* over the years. I was lucky enough to catch him at home. I told him I wanted to see him as soon as I got to town and he agreed.

"I was sitting here mourning for you," he said.

I could visualize him, an enormously fat man, wheezing over a black cigarillo that dangled between his lips, watching his television set and eating something, probably something sweet. He looked like anything but a man of action until action was called for. I might be needing him.

Beth Ryan was still out on the lawn with the boxer dog beside her when I headed for my car. I told her I was headed for New York by way of the airport.

"You planning to go back to town?" I asked her.

"I have to try to make some order out of J. W.'s papers and notes here," she said.

"I'm going to need every scrap of information you have that relates to Capra," I said.

"Most of it's in the New York office," she said. "You know about everything that's here, Peter."

Files full of dead ends, that's what I knew about.

"I'd like to go over the New York material with you tomorrow, tomorrow night," I said.

"I'll drive down first thing in the morning," she said. "I'll be at the office or at my apartment. My number is in the book."

I reached down and stroked Digger's head. I didn't know it then, but I was making a friend I was going to be very glad for later on.

The Bartram airport wasn't much to look at. There was a long macadam runway with some sheds and an office off to one side. The sheds were used for hangars for private planes and a few of the company's "taxi" jobs. Some smaller planes were staked down and covered with tarpaulins across the way. There was a flagpole sporting an American flag and some sort of pennant that represented Bartram. Over a small office building was a television aerial.

The place was busier than normal, I thought. There were three state police cars pulled up by the hangars and the parking lot was filled. People had come to rubberneck.

The focal point for everyone was the hangar where

J. W. had kept his Beachcraft Baron. I headed for it and was stopped at the open doors by a trooper.

"No one inside," he said.

I could see other troopers and several children in the semi-darkness of the interior.

"I'd like to talk to whoever's in charge," I said. "My name is Peter Styles."

That seemed to ring a bell with the trooper and he called out "Captain Garner!" Garner was a rather typical, hard-faced, unsmiling man, wearing tinted, wire-rimmed glasses which I suspected were a guard against the sunlight and not to improve his eyesight.

"We just got the word a few minutes ago that you weren't on the plane," he said.

"Last minute piece of luck," I said. I explained what had happened.

Garner's lips tightened. "We've got Jerome Colmer inside there," he said.

I looked past him and recognized Jerry sitting on a bench at the far end of the hangar, his face buried in his hands.

"Travers's son-in-law, right?" Garner asked.

I nodded.

"He was seen here in the hangar about an hour before Travers's plane took off. We've checked his fingerprints against what we can find in here."

"I don't get it," I said.

"That bomb was obviously placed on the plane here in this hangar," Garner said. "I understand Colmer wasn't on good terms with his wife or the family."

"Marriages go through that sort of thing," I said.

"Colmer's fingerprints are all over some tools on the workbench in there. He'd have needed tools to plant that bomb."

One of the things I tell myself I have, as a reporter, is an instinct for the truth when I hear it, for guilt or innocence when I confront it. I would have bet anything that Jerry Colmer hadn't set a bomb on that plane, not with his wife and two kids as passengers. Maybe he hadn't expected them to be along, but he'd seen them arrive at the airport. If he'd known they were going to be blown up, I felt certain he'd have kept them from boarding the plane.

"Is he under arrest?" I asked Colmer.

"We're holding him for questioning until the state's attorney gets here."

"What's his story?" I asked.

Garner shrugged. "He flew a Cub up here that belongs to his wife, he says. Landed about seven-thirty. That gave him an hour to do whatever he did. He said there was something wrong with the engine on the Cub. He wanted to fix it before he left it for his wife. He was familiar with this hangar. I guess when everything was jake in the family he flew the Baron quite often. He knew where tools were kept, he says. He says he fixed whatever was wrong with the Cub, replaced the tools, and took off."

"You don't buy that?"

"I'm not paid to buy explanations," Garner said. "We've got facts. I need to know a lot more before I kiss him goodbye."

"You say he was seen here in the hangar?"

"Ed Wells, one of the pilots who flies taxi out of here, saw Colmer come out of this hangar a little after eight, not long before you all arrived to take off for Boston."

"Before Steve Meadows, J. W.'s pilot, arrived?"

"We're never going to know that, are we?" Garner said. "Meadows is garbage in the fields around Framingham.

He'll never be able to tell us." He shrugged. "Colmer says he talked to Meadows, but who knows?"

"Has he got a lawyer?" I asked.

"Gave him the chance to make a phone call," Garner said. "He acts like in a shock, you know? Claims he didn't know what had happened till we told him."

"He may not have," I said. "I was with him for about three hours after the plane took off. Neither of us knew what had happened. I heard on the radio, when I was driving back into Bartram from Colmer's cottage, that I was dead!"

"We got the passenger list from Mrs. Travers. She didn't know you'd backed off at the last minute. How is she taking it?"

"Husband, daughter, two grandchildren; how would you take it?"

There was a faint glitter behind the tinted glasses. "I'd be out to kill somebody," the trooper captain said.

"That's how she's taking it," I said. "Can I talk to Colmer?"

"Until the state's attorney gets here," Garner said.

Beyond us in the windowless shed, or hangar, the afternoon sun wasn't penetrating. There was a string of four bare electric light bulbs suspended from the ceiling which gave the place a kind of cold glare.

I walked over to the bench where Jerry Colmer was sitting. He didn't stir when I spoke his name, just sat there, bent forward, his hands covering his face. I saw the residue of ink stains on his fingers, the result of the troopers taking his prints.

"It might help to talk, Jerry," I said.

Slowly, he took his hands away from his face and they shook as if he had palsy. "Oh, it's you," he said. His eyes were swollen and red. He turned his face away. "Oh, Jesus!" His whole body was contorted by some kind of spasm. "They loved to fly. They had no fear at all."

"The children?"

He nodded. "Who can have done it to them, Peter?"

"Someone out to get J. W.," I said. "Someone who knew he was going to Boston and why."

"Why was he going to Boston?"

"To talk to a man named Hardesty who grew up in Vickers Creek, knows the town, the people."

"Oh God, Oh God, Oh God, will we never get away from Vickers Creek!"

"You can't, Jerry, because that's where all this began. Somebody didn't want J. W. to get closer to the truth about what happened in that town."

He turned to me. "You know those silly, bastard troopers think I may have done it?"

"You need a lawyer, Jerry. Did Sam Tyler catch up with you?"

"No."

"He left Travers Hill to find you and tell you what had happened. We thought you might not know, unless you'd happened to turn on your radio."

"I didn't. The troopers came about ten minutes after you'd left. They told me, and they brought me down here, took my fingerprints, and said they thought I'd done it—set the bomb. How crazy can you get? My wife, my kids!"

"What did happen here?" I asked him.

"I left LaGuardia, where the Cub was hangared, about six-thirty," he said. "It takes about an hour from New York in that little plane. I landed on the strip out there. Didn't seem to be anyone around. The Cub's engine was quite uneven on the way up. I figured the gas filter was clogged. I thought I better take it out and clean it before someone else tried to fly it and it conked out. I know this place well. When things were—were different—I used to fly the Baron for J. W. I knew where tools were kept in this hangar. I thought there might even be a new filter here that would fit the Cub. I came in here, got the tools I needed, did the job."

"And saw no one? There is a pilot named Ed Wells—"

"I know Ed. I didn't happen to see him." Jerry moistened his lips. "Just as I was putting the tools away Steve Meadows came in. Steve is an old friend—was an old friend. I told him I thought I would fix the Cub. He told me he was flying J. W. and the rest to Boston in about fifteen minutes. I—I didn't want to talk to Janet on the go like that, so I took off. You all came in just as I was leaving the parking lot."

"Unfortunately, Meadows can't back up that story."

"It doesn't matter, Peter. I couldn't care less. It doesn't matter what happens now. If they say I did it, that's that."

"Wrong. It matters. Let the police wrap up the case with you in the middle of it and the people who are really responsible will walk away whistling Dixie."

"What people?"

As if he didn't know! "The same people who threw mud at Janet and murdered Jefferson Fry," I said.

He drew a deep, shuddering breath. "How can I help?" he asked.

"By getting yourself clear of this mess. I'll get Sam Tyler to you. Don't talk to the cops, or the prosecutor, or anyone else until Sam's here to help. Framing you for what's happened would be just another successful dirty trick, Jerry."

"Are you telling me that Loring Industries—?"

"I'm telling you that Death is their kind of dirty trick and that they're masters of the art," I said.

I called Sam Tyler from the airport office. He was back at Travers Hill. He'd gone to the cottage, found Jerry missing but his car still there.

"Can Jerry have gone off his rocker far enough to—to—?"

"No chance. But it would be a nice solution for Capra and company," I said. "You may find yourself up against more clout than you might expect, Sam."

"Right now, something positive to do will be a pleasure," he said.

"J. W.'s way, not Marilyn's," I said.

The drive to New York seemed interminable. I kept the car radio on, tuned to the CBS running news show. Every fifteen minutes they came back to what was now being called "the assassination of J. W. Travers." J. W. had been a defender, not a prosecutor, and yet they kept saying he must have made many enemies during his colorful legal career. The police had no leads. There was a small reference to Janet's difficulties in Vickers Creek, handled gently, as if death entitled her to that small courtesy. There was no mention of Loring Industries. J. W. had accused them openly in the trial at Vickers Creek, but to even hint that they had any connection with the bombed out plane at this point would have been grounds for a massive libel suit.

It was twilight when I garaged my car and went to my apartment off Irving Place. It was still painful for me to go back to the apartment after a time away. Grace and I had lived there, loved there. The three rooms, the kitchen and bath, the little back garden, were filled with memories of her. I had told myself over and over that I should move out of it, that I should find myself a fresh place with no vestiges of Grace in it. Somehow I couldn't.

There is an answering service attached to my phone. You ring, and you hear my voice saying I'm out but I'll get back to you if you'll leave a name and number when you hear the buzz signal. The messages go on tape.

There was one from Frank Devery to call him at home. There was a similar one from Greg Maxvil, my Manhattan Homicide friend. Most interesting was one from Virgil Hardesty, the Harvard professor from Vickers Creek, asking me to call him back. I answered that one first.

"Thank you for calling, Mr. Styles," he said, when I got through to him.

"I hope you had more on your mind than to congratulate me on being alive," I said.

"What a ghastly business!" he said.

"J. W. was counting a lot on you, Mr. Hardesty."

"I think you and I should get together," he said.

"Fine. Where and when?"

"How is your telephone, Mr. Styles?"

"What do you mean, how is it?"

"I have every reason to believe mine is tapped," Hardesty said.

Interesting. I'd been away for a week. Anything could have happened to my phone in that time.

"You hadn't thought of it, I see," Hardesty said. "I can come to New York. Be there by midnight. Is there a place—?"

"Call me at The Players Club," I said. I gave him the number. "I'll be there or there'll be a message for you."

If my phone was bugged, the people listening would know, from my conversation with Hardesty that I would at least suspect it from now on. I would get my friend Joe

Steiger, the private eye, to go over the place tomorrow and check it out.

I left the apartment and walked around the corner to The Players. The bar there was crowded with friends and acquaintances, but I skipped them and went to the phone booth at the rear where I called Frank Devery.

"So you made it," Frank said.

I told him about my call to Hardesty and the suggestion that my phone was tapped.

"More than likely," Frank said. "Does it occur to you, chum, that information leaks from everywhere?"

"Meaning?"

"How did someone know that J. W. Travers was flying to Boston in his own plane?"

"Everyone in the household at Travers Hill knew that, of course," I said.

"The bomb is set on the plane to go off when the pilot tries to contact Logan Airport on his radio," Frank said. "Whoever set the bomb knew J. W. was going to Boston. If he'd been going to land in New York or Chicago the pilot would have used a different frequency to get landing instructions and the bomb wouldn't have gone off. You see what I'm getting at? J. W. gave away his plans on a tapped phone, or someone in the household passed along the information."

"He talked to Hardesty on the phone from Travers Hill," I said. "If Hardesty's phone is bugged—"

"Or if the phone at Travers Hill is bugged. . . ." When I didn't respond to that Frank went on. "You're a trusting soul, Peter. You're one of the few men I know who doesn't have a price. Other people do, and when the buyer can afford to pay in telephone numbers, a buyer like Capra, who can you be sure of? What about the household at Travers Hill?"

"Wiped out," I said. "J. W., Janet, the two kids, Meadows, the pilot. That leaves only Marilyn in the family."

"Others, regulars there?" Frank asked.

It was hard to think of any of the others as traitors, spies for an enemy. Charles and Helen Shay, the couple, had been with J. W. for twenty-five years, trustworthy people who loved their employers; Sam Tyler, partner, lifelong friend; Al Bostick, a bodyguard whom J. W. had trusted with his life; Beth Ryan, a private secretary, probably in love with J. W.; none of them, surely, could be doubted for an instant. There were a couple of men who did the outdoor work around the place. I didn't know them.

"You don't like the idea?" Frank said.

"There was no secret about J. W.'s going to Boston," I said. "Meadows could have mentioned it to someone at the airport. It could have become public knowledge any number of ways."

"Or a way Capra has bought and paid for ever since Vickers Creek," Frank said. "He doesn't get his information on the basis of chance or luck. He buys it."

A bugged phone, I kept insisting to myself. A phony repairman at some point who hadn't been suspected. Surely not a trusted friend or employee.

"You know the local cops suspect the son-in-law?" Frank asked.

"Yes. I talked to him just before I left. Sam Tyler's taking care of him."

"He already has him out on bail, if you haven't heard," Frank said. "You don't think he's a possibility?"

"No."

"What are you, for Christ's sake, some kind of Pollyanna?" Frank asked. He sounded angry. "Any kind of decent reporter suspects everyone till they prove out. This is big league stuff, chum, not a family soap opera."

"Have you located Capra?" I asked him.

"You asked me to, didn't you? Mr. Stanley J. Capra—do you know what the J. stands for?"

"No."

"Mr. Stanley J. Capra has been very public for the last three days. You ever hear of the Golden Bough Club?"

"Some fancy place out on the Island," I said.

"I'll say it's fancy," Frank said. "Two championship eighteen-hole golf courses, saltwater and freshwater swimming pools, gold faucets in the shower baths, they tell me, tennis courts, squash courts, bars, a gourmet restaurant, horseback riding trails and stables, a polo field. You name it, the Golden Bough has it. Capra has a duplex apartment in New York, houses all over the map, red carpets available at the best hotels in the world, but he and his lady are staying at the Golden Bough, visible to hundreds of stinkingly rich friends and business associates. Why so public, you may ask? You stay public when you're engineering a private murder, is my answer. You want to live in luxury for a couple of days?"

"You're suggesting?"

"I've arranged a guest card for you at the Golden Bough."

"Why?"

Frank's voice sounded harsh. "Because there's one place where no one will take a pot shot at you, where you won't have an accident, where the food won't poison you—not while Stanley J. Capra is in residence. The Golden Bough is, right at this minute, the safest place on earth for you to be."

"You think I'm a target?"

"You're the last person left to fight the good fight, aren't you?" Frank asked. "I'm telling you, Peter, you're up against a well-organized, smoothly run, army of bastards. You're already irritating them and sooner or later they will have had it. I'll be able to use that obituary I wrote."

"Capra will know who I am."

"Of course, you idiot. I'd expect you to play it right out in the open. A good reporter goes directly to his story, doesn't he? Capra may think you're a damn fool, but he'll let you alone while you're both under the same roof. You may have a chance to unearth something out there, in that temporarily safe place, that you won't have walking the city streets, looking down dark alleys."

It was a far-out idea but it just might produce something.

"Where is the guest card?" I asked.

"Waiting for you at the desk out at the Golden Bough." Frank's laugh was humorless. "You head out there now you'll be in time for a late supper of quail's eggs and champagne. You may eat and drink *Newsview* into bankruptcy, but you'll be alive and well and living in Paris, so to speak."

I tried from that same phone booth to reach Virgil Hardesty in Boston with the idea of putting him off for a day or so. He didn't answer his phone this time. The chances were he'd already taken off for his trip to New York. I made arrangements for a room to be held for him at The Players as my guest, and I left him a message telling him that I'd been called out of town on the story we were both concerned with and that I'd get through to him at breakfast time in the morning. I didn't really know what Hardesty had, but he seemed to think it could be helpful. Right now anything at all would be gratefully received.

I suppose I have lived most of my professional life, from the time I was changed from a flippant commentator on the city's night life to an almost fanatical investigator of the climate of violence, in some kind of personal physical danger. Reporters for all the areas of the media, press, radio, television, have a certain insurance. If anything happens to one of them which appears to be retaliation by criminals, a whole army of reporters, backed by all the power of the newspapers, radio stations, and television networks sets out to identify the person or persons responsible and see to it that the law deals with them to the limit. You can get chopped down if you're caught with your head in the wrong closet, but organized crime won't risk its own neck for the sake of revenge or punishment against a newsman. They are businessmen, not emotionally-motivated hysterics. I could suspect and sniff around Stanley Capra till I ran out of energy. It would annoy and irritate him, but I'd be safe until I found myself in a position to lift the lid off the pot which would reveal what was really cooking. If I was close to that pot I didn't know where it was.

The Golden Bough is hard to believe. It is about an hour by car from New York on the ocean side of Long Island. Its members don't waste that kind of time getting there. There is a private helicopter service from the city that gets them to their special magic world in a matter of minutes. It's hard to believe and it's hard to describe, because the physical details whittle it down. There are more than a dozen buildings, including the main club-house which houses two restaurants—an elegant main dining room and a grill room—card rooms, game rooms, a billiard room, a library. There is a gymnasium where overweight millionaires pull at weights, toss medicine balls, work out on exercise tables, steam out their juices in pine-scented hot rooms, are massaged by Swedish experts, lie under sunlamps controlled by alarm systems that prevent them from overcooking, and a sleeproom where they recover from the delightful exhaustion of it all.

There are stables, and the golf club, and the beach cabanas from which you could swim in the thermostatically-controlled saltwater and freshwater pools, or go down to the beach and the ocean surf. This whole area is dotted with brightly-colored sun umbrellas. The golf courses stretch out, green, manicured to the perfection of Turkish rugs, the rough not too difficult for millionaires who hate double bogies almost as much as they hate taxes, the white sand in the traps sifted to the texture of fine salt, punctuating the landscape.

There are hangars for the helicopters, boathouses for the power boats, the stables as elegant as the average hotels for humans, fenced in riding rings, and soft-earth riding trails leading off into the woods.

The membership of the Golden Bough is not large. Who can afford it? The cost makes it exclusive. For people who want to stay, there are four residence buildings broken up into two-room apartments, each with a kitchenette. Most of the millionaires don't come there without female companions, but those who do are sent to a dormitory building with single rooms and communal baths and showers. There is a kind of tropical look to the white buildings with their red tile roofs.

All these structures, all the facilities for a great variety of recreation, don't really tell the story. I arrived at the gates that shut off the Golden Bough from the rest of the world about eleven o'clock that night. A man in a navy-blue uniform came to the car window.

"Mr. Styles?" he asked, before I could tell him.

I admitted I was.

"Your guest card is waiting for you in the entrance hall, sir," the man said. "If I may ride up to the club house with you, I'll garage your car."

He went around and got into the passenger seat beside me. He said it had been a nice day. I said it had, though it had been one of the worst days I could remember except for two others. Five people were violently dead, four of whom I knew well and cared for, and the man most probably responsible was just a few yards up this impeccable bluestone driveway.

"Will you be wanting your car early in the morning?" the man asked, as we pulled up under the clubhouse portico.

"I have no plans yet for the morning," I told him.

He took my bag out of the back seat. Instantly there was a red-coated bellboy there to take it.

"Anything in the trunk, sir?"

I wasn't the average guest, I guess. No golf clubs, no other sporting equipment. Just an overnight bag. I followed the bellboy into what I hesitate to call the "lobby." It was an elegant reception hall. There were paintings by some of the better French impressionists, a huge fireplace at one end, a giant picture window which I guessed overlooked the ocean. There wasn't much in the way of furniture. You didn't live in this room, you just passed through it.

A man in an elegant dinner jacket came out of an inner room to greet me. "We've been expecting you, Mr. Styles," he said. "I'm Wainwright." He looked past me as if he expected to see someone else. "You're alone?"

"Quite alone," I said.

"Show Mr. Styles to apartment B in the Crampton House," Wainwright said to the bellboy. "If someone plans to join you later, Mr. Styles, they'll be informed here where to find you."

His face was deadpan, but I knew he was talking about a woman.

"Don't I have to sign a register?" I asked.

"No, sir," Wainwright said. "You are a guest of the club."

Crampton House was just across the driveway from this main building. My quarters consisted of a bedroom, living room, kitchenette and bath on the ground floor.

"Mr. Wainwright thought you'd prefer something on the first floor, not having to deal with the stairs," the bellboy said. The bastards knew about my leg! I don't walk with a limp. A stranger wouldn't know, but they knew. Peter Styles's history had preceded him to the Golden Bough.

"Mr. Capra is in the card room," the bellboy said.

I just stared at him.

"He'd be happy to have you join him for a nightcap in the bar about midnight," the bellboy said.

I drew a deep breath. "Where is the bar?" I asked.

"In the main building where we just came from," the boy said. "Just to the left of the ocean windows."

He was waiting for something, and I recovered from the mild shock he'd sent me into and handed him a dollar bill. He didn't look happy.

Capra was expecting me. It took me a minute or two to realize it hadn't required any kind of special espionage on his part. I was news. In this one long day I had been reported dead and then resurrected. The members of the

Golden Bough Club were the kind of people who would have been interested in the violent death of J. W. Travers. Travers's clients had come from this kind of world in the past. Most of them must know about Vickers Creek and the "dirty trick" implications against Loring Industries J. W. had voiced in the courtroom there. My contact with the case would be known by anyone who read *Newsview*. When someone heard that I had been put up as a guest at the Golden Bough the news must have spread. It would certainly have been passed on to Capra in a hurry. He was taking the play away from me. He was moving first.

He would be "happy" to have me join him for a nightcap? He knew damn well I hadn't come to the Golden Bough to play paddle tennis! I was going to have a chance to look at his best curve ball before I was really set in the batter's box.

As I've said, J. W. had done an enormous amount of research on the top man in Loring Industries. I had listened to tapes and read dozens of Beth Ryan's transcripts of other tapes I didn't get to hear. What did I know about Stanley J. Capra beyond the central fact of his power? According to *The Wall Street Journal,* Loring Industries, in the second quarter of this year, had announced profits that exceeded a record set by Exxon a year ago—far beyond a billion dollars; what Frank Devery called "telephone numbers." That was naked power, right out in public view. Loring Industries could, if it had chosen to, have saved a struggling fellow giant like Chrysler and felt it no more than Capra himself would have felt a five dollar tip to a hatcheck girl. Governments around the world tipped their hats to Stanley Capra, who sat at the controls of Loring Industries. He could provide you with anything you needed, at his price of course—guns, butter, oil, votes, cooperation. Kings and presidents stood aside while Stanley J. Capra walked through the door first.

But what about the man himself? Everything had fallen into place for Stanley Capra in the neatest kind of order. His father, Jason Capra—is that what the J. stood for?—had been one of the so-called "robber barons," one of the giants who had turned the free-enterprise system into a private gold mine. Stanley had come into the world with more money already deposited in his name than it was easy to imagine. If he had chosen he could have gone through life without ever indulging in anything but the pleasures that money can buy: houses, women, what have you. Stanley, however, inherited from his father a lust for power. Jason Capra had been interested in two solid facts, oil and steel. It was Stanley who added railroads and airlines and newspapers and radio and television networks and, most recently, nuclear power plants to the Loring empire. That just scratched the surface. There were so many things that would not appear in an audit of the company's books, things they owned, like congressmen and senators and princes and revolutionary leaders of the Third World who shout their allegiance to the "people" and actually eat them alive.

Money created the American aristocracy a hundred years ago. You hear about people whose ancestors "came over on the Mayflower," but in the end the great families were the rich families. Some of the founders of the "first families" were on the crude side, like Jason Capra. Other families, not so rich perhaps, had taken on the gloss and sheen of social elegance. Among such families were the Markhams of Newport and Park Avenue. In his drive to the top, it was quite logical that Stanley Capra should woo and win Nancy Markham, combining the best of two worlds—the world of ruthless power and the world of social elegance. Nancy, a patrician beauty, had polished the rough edges off Stanley, and Stanley had made her a queen. The one flaw in what everyone said was a "perfect marriage" was their failure to have children. There was backroom talk that after the first few years of the marriage Stanley Capra had become a "closet" womanizer. He was cool about it, never seen anywhere with any gal but his wife. J. W. had said that, like the sailor who has a woman in every port, Stanley Capra had a woman in every big city in the world. J. W. had thought it might be a way to get at Capra, but as far as I knew he hadn't come up with anything useable.

I had seen Capra quite a few times before that night, but never to be introduced to him or speak to him. I had covered political rallies and fundraising drives where he'd been a key figure and speaker. I'd seen him interviewed on television. He must be sixty now, I thought; a big man, physically fit, with iron-gray hair and an almost perpetual smile. He would be attractive to women, even to much younger women. According to Frank Devery, Nancy Capra was here at the Golden Bough with her husband. Stanley wouldn't be playing any woman games here.

Just before midnight I walked across the yard to the main building. In the reception hall I could hear the soft sound of a small string orchestra. It wasn't canned music. Wainwright appeared as if he'd been watching my approach on a monitor. I got the notion that I couldn't move anywhere around this place without someone knowing where I was. Orders from Capra?

"The bar is just through that door to your left, Mr. Styles," Wainwright said. He knew where I was going. "Are your quarters satisfactory?"

"Fine," I said.

"Anything you want," he said, giving me a wry little smile. He was talking about women again.

The bar was a large, dimly-lit room. Three or four couples, all in evening clothes, sat at tables. No sign of Capra. I felt a little out of place in my dark blue tropical worsted summer suit. You dressed for the evening at the Golden Bough.

The music was pleasantly audible there, though I had no idea where it originated.

I went to the bar. A red-coated bartender gave me a cheerful smile. "Jack Daniels on the rocks, Mr. Styles?" He knew what I drank. I had the uncomfortable feeling that he could tell me what kind of underwear I had on. These people knew everything there was to know about me it seemed.

I sipped the whiskey on the rocks he brought me. "I guess you could say this has been your lucky day," he said. "The early news about you was bad."

I just nodded and stayed with my drink.

"I guess if you have to go it's best if it's unexpected and quick," the bartender said.

"Not for the people you leave behind who care for you," I said.

"J. W. Travers was a guest here quite a few times," the bartender said. "Seemed like a really nice gentleman, and, from all accounts, one of the smartest."

"Not smart enough to have seen what was aimed his way," I said. "I'm supposed to be a very smart reporter, but I'm not smart enough to see what's aimed my way. Can you give me any hints?"

"I don't get you," he said.

"You knew in advance what I drink. Maybe you know what else I can expect."

He laughed, as though he was suddenly relaxed. "The Jack Daniels? We pride ourselves on being a step ahead of our guests," he said. "No secret about it, Mr. Styles. You're a famous man. You've been in the news all day. Wainwright knew late today you were going to be a guest. I had watched the news, you know? When I was told to expect you I remembered this morning, when they thought you'd gone down with that plane, they mentioned things about you. They said you were a member of The Players. Richard, the bartender there, is an old friend of mine. I called him and asked him what you drank. He told me, always Jack Daniels on the rocks. We try to make our guests feel at home, you know?"

I was aware that someone had come up beside me at the bar, a square, rugged-looking gent in his fifties, dark hair, dark eyes, mahogany-tanned, wearing a wine-colored dinner jacket with a wine-colored tie and cummerbund.

"Mr. Styles? I'm Ben Martin, an associate of Mr. Capra," he said. "If you'd care to join us at a table—?"

I turned and saw Capra and another man, both in conventional black dinner jackets, standing by a circular table in a far corner of the room. Capra was smiling at me as though I was a long-lost friend. I was torn between him and getting a closer look at Ben Martin. Martin had been mentioned on several of J. W.'s tapes about Loring Industries. "The master of the Dirty Tricks Department," J. W. had called him. J. W. had been certain that the framing of Janet at Vickers Creek was the kind of thing Ben Martin would have conceived.

"The man with Mr. Capra is Curtis Bond," Martin said, as we started to move toward the table. "You could call him Mr. Capra's chief of staff. His official title is Vice President in charge of Communications—our newspapers, radio stations, TV networks. Super-publicity man, I suppose you'd say."

Curtis Bond was younger than the other two, militarily erect, sandy hair crew cut, pale grey eyes, alert like a fighter waiting to see where the next punch might be coming from.

Capra held out a hand in greeting as we reached him. "I've never had the pleasure of meeting you, Styles," he said, in a low, almost musical voice, "but I feel as if I've known you a long time. Constant reader, you might say." His handshake was firm. "I don't think you've met Curtis Bond."

Bond gave me a brief nod, no move toward a handshake. We sat down around the table. A waiter had appeared out of nowhere.

"The usual, Emmet," Capra said. "And you, Styles?"

"Another Jack Daniels?" the waiter asked. He was primed.

Capra fished a cigarette out of a silver case and Bond promptly held a lighter for him. Service, even from vice presidents.

"This must have been a pretty staggering day for you," Capra said. He actually sounded sympathetic.

"A very lucky day," I said. "Until the very last minute I was supposed to be on that plane."

"So I understand. You know, Styles, I don't think you and I should beat around the bush. It will save us both a lot of time."

"What bush?" I asked.

"Shall we—let down our hair?" His smile was almost blinding. "You were a close friend of J. W. Travers. You were a house guest as of this morning. You were planning to take a plane trip with him to Boston."

All that, of course, had been in and on the news.

"The logical place for a good friend to be at this moment," he went on, "is with the grieving widow. I feel for Marilyn, I really do. A charming woman, and I know how deeply she cared for J. W. But you, a friend and cohort, leave her and get yourself a guest card here at the Golden Bough. You come, I'm told, with a small overnight bag. You are obviously not planning to golf or play tennis or ride. You've come here because I'm here. Am I right, Styles?"

"Sidestepping the bush, the answer is yes," I said.

"I like the direct approach," Capra said. He glanced, smiling at his two cohorts, as though he was saying "I told you so." They had obviously discussed how to handle me, and they were doing it Capra's way, over what may have been objections from the others. How to handle Peter Styles! The bastards!

"Let me save you some probing and probably ineffectual questions, Styles," Capra said. "Shall we go back to Vickers Creek? I know you covered the case there."

"You've chosen to make the first move," I said.

"There is an unfortunate syndrome in this country today," Capra said, "that leads people to believe that big companies that make big profits on paper are necessarily evil. Some time back Exxon showed a profit for one quarter of over a billion dollars. People immediately screamed for an excess profit tax. Our government benignly promised that that tax money would go to searching for new sources of energy. Well, where do you think it goes now? Into the pockets of the top men? It goes back into the ground, searching for new sources of energy with skills the government hasn't got and will never have. When Loring Industries, a few months back, showed an even larger profit for a quarter, the people, who don't know what they're talking about, cried "Evil!"

again. Our profits go into nuclear energy. The government wouldn't know how to proceed with such a program if they put us out of business."

He spoke with something like an evangelical passion.

"The outcries from radicals against big business are the mouthings of know-nothings," he went on. "The development of new sources of energy spells survival for this country and for the free-enterprise system. The outcries of a black radical like Jefferson Fry or a hysterical girl like Janet Colmer, J. W.'s daughter, are pebbles thrown against a brick wall. Do you think anything they could do or say against the carefully planned and executed procedures of Loring Industries could do us the smallest piece of harm, Styles?"

"If enough people were aroused—"

"Nonsense," he said sharply. "Oh, they might keep Curtis here busy feeding the general public with truth, raise our budget for public relations. But enough harm for us to plan a murder and blacken—if you'll forgive what may sound like a play on words—the reputation of a silly girl? Enough harm to justify our taking such risks? That is a completely absurd notion, Styles. J. W. Travers, a highly intelligent man, was driven beyond reason by his emotional daughter. He believed her without going after the real facts, which he would have done in any other circumstances. What good could it do Loring Industries to make it appear that Janet Travers Colmer was screwing a black man?"

"It could shut her up."

"Stop her from shouting from the roof tops that we were evil? That wasn't doing us any damage, Styles. Jefferson Fry wasn't doing us any damage. Like I said, pebbles tossed against a brick wall."

"So what did happen in Vickers Creek?"

"Just what appeared on the surface," Capra said. "The townspeople resented the appearance of strangers making noisy demonstrations against a project that was supplying hundreds of jobs for their neighbors. It's a small southern town with an old-fashioned prejudice against black agitators. The local sheriff got a warrant for the arrest of the leaders on a charge of malicious mischief. He broke into Fry's motel room and found him in the hay with Janet Colmer. Fry resisted arrest and was shot when he attacked a deputy. Nothing more than that, Styles. Nothing behind it, no 'dirty tricks' by an evil corporation as J. W. suggested in court. Why should there have been? They couldn't do us an ounce of harm. Why should we have involved ourselves in a melodramatic, Watergate kind of garbage? I know you've been working for months on this thing with J. W. Have you come up with a shred of evidence to link Loring Industries with what happened there? I know you've had a private detective snooping around Vickers Creek for weeks and weeks. Has he come up with anything? Of course he hasn't, because there isn't anything for him to find."

Unfortunately what Capra was saying was true. J. W. and I had believed, were certain, but so far there was no proof.

"And now I come to today," Capra said, and his smile was gone. "I know you, Styles. I know how your mind works. I've followed your writings in *Newsview* for years. You are a man who believes in the conspiracy of big power. Well, I admit it, I am big power, Styles. You leave a bereaved woman to come here to the Golden Bough because I am here, and because you believe J. W.'s hogwash about Vickers Creek. I can read your mind as though it was passing across your forehead on a news-ticker tape. The head of the evil corporation has plotted the death of the honest lawyer who was out to get him. You came here because you think I am responsible for the bomb that blew up that plane over Boston and got rid of my enemy. That is childish, Styles; utterly childish. If there was evidence that would incriminate me in the Vickers Creek business, J. W.'s death wouldn't hide it, would it? The evidence wouldn't be something he carried in his watch pocket, would it? You would know what it is, his partners would know what it is, his wife would know what it is. And if I wiped you all out, it would still be there for someone else to find, wouldn't it? How can I convince you that I had nothing to do with Vickers Creek and that I certainly, before God, had nothing to do with that dreadful business today?"

Eloquence he had. Reasonable men would believe him. I guess I'm just not a reasonable man. Every warning instinct I have told me I was being sold a plausible bill of goods.

"As a reporter it's my job to examine every possible angle of a case," I said. "The truth is all that matters to me, Capra."

"I've been telling you the truth," he said.

"When I'm convinced of it I'll be out of your hair," I said.

His smile came back. "It's late. I've had too damn much fresh air today. I need sleep. In the morning I'll answer any questions you may have, arrange to have you see any books or records. Will that do?"

"That will be fine," I said.

The waiter tapped me on the shoulder. "A phone call for you, Mr. Styles."

We all rose. It was agreed I would meet Capra after breakfast in the lounge. I went to the phone in a booth at the end of the bar. The only person who knew I was at the Golden Bough was Devery, not counting Capra's army, of course.

"Peter?" Devery's voice had the sound of trouble.

"Frank, this is a place with very long ears," I said.

"I just want to tell you some news that's just come over the ticker and which will be on your TV set if you've got one in your room."

"Fire when ready," I said.

"A Harvard professor named Virgil Hardesty checked into the Hotel Beaumont about an hour and a half ago," Frank said. "Ten minutes later, according to the police, he took a swan dive out of a fourteenth-floor window and is hamburger on the sidewalk. Suicide, they say."

Hardesty had never gotten my message, never turned up at The Players. He'd checked into a hotel first and never been able to leave.

"Suicide my foot!" I heard Devery say.

PART TWO

1

Ben Martin, the dark, powerfully-built vice president in charge of dirty tricks, was hovering outside the phone booth when I emerged.

"Nothing wrong, I hope," he said.

I could feel a kind of anger beginning to boil inside me that reminded me of other dark times. I was a bug under a microscope to these jerks. They knew about my past, they knew what I liked to drink, and Capra had said he could read my mind like the tape from a news ticker. And he had known exactly what I was thinking, damn him. I was prepared to bet that while he and this Martin creep and the crew-cut Curtis Bond sat at that circular table with me, showing me how much they knew about me, they had been perfectly well aware that Professor Virgil Hardesty was on his way from Boston to New York; over his tapped phone they had learned that he'd made a reservation at the Hotel Beaumont and made certain that Hardesty and I would never meet.

"I suspect the girl on the switchboard can tell you about it," I said to Martin.

Wainwright was waiting for me in the reception hall.

"I've ordered your car up, Mr. Styles," he said.

You can't beat the service at the Golden Bough—nor the efficiency of its eavesdropping. They knew just how I would react to the news they'd known I was going to get. You want to feel helpless, play games with the likes of Stanley J. Capra. He knew every move you would make before you knew you were going to have to make it. That ought to persuade you to give up.

Well, screw him!

I left the Golden Bough just before two in the morning. The expressway was clear of traffic at that hour and I made good time, glancing in my rearview mirror rather frequently. I halfway expected to find I was being tailed, but I suppose that would have been a little crude for Capra. There'd be someone waiting outside my garage on Irving Place to pick me up, if knowing where I went was important to them. Maybe, like in a science fiction movie, the president and the two vice presidents of Loring Industries were watching me on some kind of magic monitor that would tell them what I was up to around the clock. That kind of junk thinking was the effect they had on me at the moment.

I didn't go to my usual place. I parked my car in the garage across the street from the Algonquin Hotel on Forty-fourth Street. I called Devery from the Algonquin lobby.

"We got lucky," Frank told me. "Maxvil's in charge of the Hardesty business. He'll turn up here at my apartment when he can. Join me here. I've got a double-double waiting for you."

Greg Maxvil, my friend on Manhattan Homicide, is a new breed of cop, a man with a law degree and a complete knowledge of all the most modern scientific techniques of crime fighting. He is a trim, steel-wire kind of man with restless, penetrating dark eyes that appear able to read the label on the inside of your shirt collar. He is a cultivated gent who reads, knows and appreciates good painting, likes classical music and ballet. He's a charming companion when he isn't working. When he is working he is tough and relentless. New York, he thinks, is the capital of the world. Sooner or later all the big fish of crime will drift into his jurisdiction. He waits for them, ready. As Frank said, we were lucky to have Greg on our side in any segment of this multiple horror story.

The count was up to six now; six violently dead people in less than twenty-four hours.

Maxvil had already arrived at Frank Devery's Beekman Place apartment when I got there. I was relieved to see him.

"Hairbreadth Harry," he said to me. "You escape a bomb in a plane and you escape a meeting with your friend from Boston. You might have gone out a window with him if you'd managed to meet."

"It was murder?" I asked.

Maxvil was stretched in a comfortable armchair, a drink in one hand, a cigarette in the other. He's a chain smoker in spite of endless warnings from Devery, who sucks on empty pipes and unlit cigars trying to shake the habit.

"I wangled my way onto the case on the chance that it may be," Maxvil said. "J. W. Travers was on his way to see Hardesty when his plane blew up. Hardesty, Frank tells me, had information Travers wanted. He plans to pass it on to you. That's enough to make the brass wonder. Personally, I have no doubt about it. But proof?" He shrugged.

Devery handed me my "double-double," which was a goblet filled with Jack Daniels poured over ice cubes. I drank a little, gratefully.

"It was a bang-bang happening," Maxvil said. "He

signed in at the Beaumont at ten minutes to eleven. Just twelve minutes later he was on the sidewalk, fourteen floors down. We've been over the room. He'd put his suitcase down on the bed and opened it, but he hadn't unpacked anything. A bellboy took him up to the room. They have a rack for luggage, but Hardesty asked the boy to put it down on the bed. No special reason. He just liked it better that way. What it suggests is that almost immediately after the bellboy left him, well tipped, by the way, someone else knocked on the door. Hardesty went to see who it was, and—the End."

"Bellboy see anyone?" Devery asked.

Maxvil rubbed out his cigarette and lit a fresh one. "People coming and going on fourteen," he said. "Boy didn't have any reason to pay attention. One thing. The boy was sure Hardesty was carrying a leather briefcase. We haven't found it." He took a deep drag on his cigarette. "I understand you've just been in the lions' den."

I told him about my extraordinary two hours at the Golden Bough, my session with Capra and his lieutenants, their complete information about me, and the last bit about their having my car ready after Devery had phoned me about Virgil Hardesty.

"They had me covered like a tent," I said.

"And Hardesty," Maxvil said. His face had taken on the hard, cold working mask I knew so well. "He told you he thought his phone was tapped?"

"And suggested maybe mine was, too," I said.

"So they knew from listening in on that conversation that he was coming to New York to pass on to you whatever it was he'd had for J. W. Travers. We know, because we checked, that he made his reservation at the Beaumont by phone, presumably from Boston. So they knew when he was going, when he got here, and when he'd arrive. Covered like a tent, as you say, Peter. They were ready for him, and they got him."

"And his briefcase," Devery said.

Devery's phone rang. He crossed the room to answer it. I glanced at my watch. It was just after four in the morning.

"For you," Devery said to Maxvil. "Headquarters."

Maxvil went to the phone. He listened for what seemed a long time, not talking himself beyond a "yes" or "no." He finally put down the phone and stood there looking at us.

"The news about Hardesty has reached Boston," he said.

"I suppose it's been all over radio and TV," Devery said.

"A friend heard it," Maxvil said. "A fellow faculty member at Harvard, one Mr. Clark Forrester. Name mean anything to you, Peter?"

"No."

"Mr. Clark Forrester is all broken up about his friend," Maxvil said, his voice cold and forebidding. "He was afraid something like this might happen. According to Mr. Clark Forrester, Virgil Hardesty has been in a suicidal frame of mind for some months. He thinks Hardesty may have been suffering from sort of terminal illness. Would you like to bet what that illness was?"

"One guesses cancer," Devery said.

"My guess is that he suffered from knowing too much about Stanley J. Capra and Loring Industries," Maxvil said. "My guess is that Mr. Clark Forrester has just been paid a handsome fee to sell us a crock full."

"Oh, brother!" Devery said.

"Mr. Clark Forrester is at the Beaumont, having shuttled down from Boston to do what he can about the 'arrangements' for his dead friend's body." Maxvil's anger was mounting. "I must go there to give him the official eye, and he will be watching very closely to see whether I buy his story. Your dirty tricks friends very much hope I will, Peter. Let there be no official connection between the violence of yesterday morning, and the sad 'suicide' of last night! Well, publicly, I do buy the suicide story. Maybe that will relax the sonsofbitches."

"I'd like to go with you," I said to Maxvil.

"Stay out of it, Peter," Devery said. "We've said it over and over. They've got you covered like a tent."

"A statement from Peter might help them believe we've swallowed it whole," Maxvil said.

"It's police work," Devery said. "Peter's useless on this story now."

"You're not going to quit, are you, Peter?" Maxvil said. "Knight on a white charger, out to keep Marilyn Travers from throwing away her life?"

"That's what'll happen," I said. "If she tries to get at Capra, there'll be another 'suicide': grief-stricken widow drives her car into a tree, or takes a high dive of her own. If we don't get Capra first they'll get her, if she asks for it."

"I think Peter can be useful," Maxvil said. "Sometimes one man can get through a hole in the fence where an army of cops can't."

"I promise to stay away from high up windows," I said to Devery.

He shook his head. "I could fire you but that wouldn't stop you, would it? You want to be a hero, that's your kind of patented idiocy!"

Devery was right, of course. I was asking for it and the odds were I would get it. But ever since the moment I'd heard the news about J. W.'s death, ever since my arrival at the Golden Bough, a slow outrage against Capra's kind of power had been cooking to a boil in me. Friends, decent people, innocent kids, wiped out as casually as someone spraying flies on a window screen. I couldn't just walk away from it to avoid being number seven. I couldn't stand by and let Marilyn Travers become another notch on the butt of Capra's gun. I couldn't stay out of it and live with myself. It was as simple as that.

I didn't intend, however, to let myself be rubbed out without making some kind of a score of my own.

Maxvil and I walked west from Beekman Place toward the Beaumont. The first grey light of dawn was visible in the sky behind us.

"You could take a vacation in the South Sea Islands," Maxvil said, not looking at me.

"If Capra wants to get me he has people anywhere, everywhere," I said. "My only chance, Greg, is to crawl through that hole in the fence you were talking about."

"But where is the fence?" he asked.

I didn't have the answer to that—yet.

"There aren't too many ways I can help you," Maxvil said, still looking straight ahead as we walked. "Suppose we find the man who set the bomb on the plane. I can almost promise you it won't lead us to Capra or Loring Industries. Suppose we find the man who tossed Hardesty out a window. He'll almost certainly turn out to be a simple hotel thief, no connection to the big boys. Finding those particular villains is police work, but finding them isn't going to produce what you want, a case against Capra."

"So Merry Christmas," I said with some bitterness.

Maxvil stopped walking to light a cigarette. He looked at me, his eyes narrowed against the sudden cloud of smoke. "If I were you—or the Lone Ranger," he said, "I'd approach this thing from a different angle."

"What angle?"

"The miserable frame-up at Vickers Creek was carefully planned, covered, untouchable even by the great J. W. Travers. The bombing was planned, covered, untouchable as far as Capra is concerned, even if we catch the bomber. Hardesty's swan dive, the same thing. You can spend your life trying to hook Capra into those ventures and you'll come up empty. They're waiting for you, ready for you. Somewhere they're not waiting for you, not ready for you."

"How do you mean?"

"Capra has a weakness somewhere," Maxvil said. "A woman? A long forgotten dirty trick used against someone, somewhere? A double cross forgotten in the swirl of passing events? That's the unprotected hole in the fence, Peter; a weak spot he's forgotten to guard because no one has moved that way. Aim at him for the frame-up in Vickers Creek, the bombing, this Hardesty business, and he has an empire gathered around him to make sure you don't make it. Hit him where he isn't looking for it and you may have a chance."

"Where do I look?"

"I wish I could tell you," Maxvil said. "I'll keep him on guard in the Hardesty case, and through connections, I'll keep the bombing investigation alive, the Vickers Creek thing simmering. I'll keep his attention focused where he's ready. Maybe you can find the hole in the fence while he's looking somewhere else—that's the only way you can win this ballgame, friend."

Wisdom from a wise man. It made sense. I was almost laughably out of control as long as I kept aiming at the obvious. My phone probably tapped, my mind almost literally read, my comings and goings watched, my personal habits, probably down to the blend of pipe tobacco I smoke, known. I was what I'd thought of myself as being out at the Golden Bough, a bug under a microscope. But if I could fade away and slip through Maxvil's hole in the fence the scales might tilt in my favor. But where and how?

Maxvil and I had reached the Beaumont and we walked into the almost deserted lobby of New York's top luxury hotel. Hardesty hadn't been looking for an inexpensive base of operations. The early morning cleaning crew were at work as we crossed toward the desk. The night clerk knew Maxvil, who'd been there earlier on.

"I suppose you've come back to talk to Forrester, Lieutenant," the clerk said. "He's in room six fourteen."

"Thanks," Maxvil said.

"Our security chief asked me to tell you he wanted to talk to you before you went anywhere else. May I call him?"

It turned out not to be necessary. Jerry Dodd, a former FBI agent who handles security for Pierre Chambrun, the almost legendary manager of the Beaumont, evidently had eyes and ears of his own. He was coming across the lobby toward us, a small, wiry man suggesting intense, pent-up energy.

"Glad I caught you, Lieutenant," he said. He nodded to me. "Good morning, Mr. Styles."

The Golden Bough didn't have too much on the Beaumont.

"About Hardesty's briefcase, Lieutenant," Dodd said to Maxvil. "I'm certain it existed. Our night bell captain was at the desk when Hardesty registered. There was a suitcase and a briefcase which Hardesty put down on the desk as he was signing his card. The bell boy who picked up his bag reached for the briefcase but Hardesty wasn't having any. 'I'll hang onto that,' he said. The clerk saw and heard that, the bell captain saw and heard it, the boy who carried the suitcase saw and heard it. There *was* a briefcase."

"I never doubted it," Maxvil said.

"The window in fourteen B through which Hardesty fell is a straight drop to the street," Dodd said. "No fire escapes, no balconies, no ledges. If Hardesty was hanging onto the briefcase when he was shoved out, it went down with him. He could easily have dropped it, clawing for safety as he fell. If the briefcase fell free, it could have taken some kind of crazy bounce if it landed just so. We've searched everywhere, even across the street. No sign of it. It's nowhere. Somebody took it."

"That's for sure," Maxvil said.

"It could have been someone passing in the street," Dodd said. "I suspect you don't believe that."

"Not for a minute," Maxvil said.

"You don't believe Forrester's suicide theory?"

Maxvil gave the security man a thin smile. "I haven't heard it yet," he said. "Until I'm convinced by him, I think the scene went this way. The bellboy carried the suitcase into fourteen B and put it down on the bed as Hardesty requested. Hardesty tipped the boy, who then left. Then Hardesty put the briefcase down, probably also on the bed, and opened his bag. Then, quickly, someone knocked or rang the doorbell."

"There is a doorbell," Dodd said.

"So, Hardesty went to the door. Someone jammed a gun in his gut, rushed him to the window, and out he went."

"No fight?"

"Maybe he was knocked cold the moment he opened the door, carried to the window, thrown out. In either case the briefcase was where he had put it down. The killer took it, walked away with it."

"You think the killer was after the briefcase?"

"And the life of the man who knew what was in it," Maxvil said. "So, now for Mr. Forrester."

"Half a dozen newspaper and media people have been here to talk to him," Dodd said. "I wondered about it because he hasn't made any calls from his room."

"I think you can depend on it that someone let the press know he was here," Maxvil said. "A long story, Dodd, which someday Peter and I may tell you."

We went up to the sixth floor and rang the bell to 614. Clark Forrester was what I would call the perfect professor type: tweed jacket, grey flannel slacks, white shirt with a red-and-blue striped tie, tan loafers. Almost a uniform. He was bone thin, his blond hair worn a little long, heavy horn-rimmed glasses covering weak-looking eyes.

Maxvil produced his badge. "Lieutenant Maxvil, in charge of the Hardesty case," he said. "This is Peter Styles of *Newsview* magazine."

"Oh my, what a terrible day for you, Mr. Styles. For all of us, you might say. Please come in, gentlemen." His voice was small, almost timid.

We followed him into the room. The gentlemen of the press had left their mark in full ashtrays. Forrester reached nervously in his pocket for a pipe and a plastic pouch.

"I came, as soon as I heard the news in Boston," he said. "My room in the dormitory at Cambridge, as a matter of fact. I knew at once things here weren't what they appeared to be."

"What did they appear to be, Mr. Forrester?" Maxvil asked.

"Murder, according to the news reports," Forrester said.

"You didn't go for that?"

Forrester got his pipe filled. He struggled with a book of paper matches and finally got it going. Now for today's lecture, I thought.

"I have been very close to Virgil for a number of years," he said. "We're both on the Liberal Arts faculty at Harvard. I teach a general course in literature, Homer to Sinclair Lewis. Virgil teaches—taught—a comprehensive history course. Brilliant scholar. But, poor guy, in the last months he wasn't himself. He never told me exactly what it was, but I assumed it was some kind of terminal illness."

"He never told you what?"

"He hinted. I assumed it was a malignancy of some sort. But he talked endlessly about not letting himself live through the agony of physical pain, or diminished capacities. I—I tried to keep a close watch on him, convinced he meant to do himself mortal harm."

"You didn't believe he had the right to do himself in if he chose?" Maxvil asked.

"The right? Oh, I think perhaps he had the right, Lieutenant. I—I might even have helped him to do it in a less ugly way than this. Pills, you know what I mean?"

"He didn't ask you to?"

"No. He wanted to be alone with his problems. But I was concerned. I thought it would happen just the way it seems to have happened."

"How was that?" Maxvil asked, deceptively mild.

"Spur of the moment," Forrester said. "I don't think Virgil could have planned it all out. An overdose of something, lie down and wait for it to happen. Maybe cut wrists in a warm bath, relaxing until it was all over. He talked about suicide once or twice, not in any emotional way. I don't even remember how it came up. But I remember his saying that he could never go through with any kind of careful suicide plan. 'I'd always turn back at the last minute; take an emetic to up-chuck the poison, apply a tourniquet to my arm to stop the bleeding. I'd be a coward if I had time to think about it.' "

"He said all that?"

"Yes," Forrester said. "It stayed with me because I was worried about him, about his preoccupation with death."

"Other friends must have been worried, too," Maxvil said.

"I don't know that he confided in anyone else. We were very close."

"But when you heard he'd gone out the window here you assumed the police, who called it murder, had made a mistake?"

"Quite sure," Forester said. His pipe had gone out and he was having great trouble with his paper matches. "It's the way I'd been sure it would happen when the time came. An instant decision: standing on the edge of a subway platform, the train coming, an action from which there was no return. Down under the wheels. I think that's what happened here. He was taken up to his room, was left by the bellboy, turned and saw the open window. Impulse. He just dove out. No time to think about it, no way to turn back. It would be completely in character."

"Do you know why Hardesty came to New York, Mr. Forrester?"

"No."

"You were so close."

"I could guess."

"Do," Maxvil said.

"I know he'd been in touch with J. W. Travers," Forrester said. "They'd been in touch about Vickers Creek, Virgil's home town. I think Travers was on his way to Boston to talk to Virgil when—when his plane blew up. I think Virgil may have come to New York to talk to Travers's partners."

"Why?" Maxvil asked.

I noticed that Forrester made a point of not looking at me. Instinct told me he knew damn well that Hardesty had come to New York to see me.

"What happened to Travers's daughter in Vickers Creek," Forrester said. "I think Virgil thought he might have information that would be useful to Travers. Travers's partner or partners would be the logical people to give it to now."

"But the open window was too much for him?"

"It must have been that way, Lieutenant."

"Couldn't wait to pass on the information he had, after going to the trouble of flying down here in the middle of the night?"

"He was deeply disturbed, Lieutenant. He saw a way out, and nothing else mattered."

"I understand you've already suggested this theory to reporters here."

Forrester nodded. "They asked to see me."

"How did they know you were here and had something to tell?" Maxvil asked.

Forrester's eyes blinked as if he didn't quite understand the question. "I—I hadn't thought about that," he said. "When I arrived here at the Beaumont I told the man at the desk I was a friend of Virgil's, that I wanted to talk to someone in charge of the case. I suppose he passed that along to the reporters."

"The man at the desk?"

"I can't think of anyone else," Forrester said.

Gift wrapped, I thought, neat and tidy.

Maxvil was dangerously polite. He thanked Forrester

for what he'd had to tell. He said it probably explained what had looked more sinister at first glance. He added that the condition of Hardesty's smashed body might make it difficult for the medical examiner to determine what his terminal illness had been. Outside in the hallway I looked at Maxvil.

"So he can report to Capra that he did his job well, that you bought his story?"

"Precisely," Maxvil said.

"But you didn't?"

Maxvil's laugh was mirthless. "The sonofabitch is a first-class liar," he said. "I know this hotel and how it operates. I'll check it out, but I'll bet a year's salary that no one here called reporters."

"If Hardesty was suicidal wouldn't other friends know?"

"I'll have a man in Boston talk to other friends," Maxvil said. "What do you think the odds are that other friends ever dreamed of it? I'd say long, longer, longest." He looked at me appraisingly. "Go get some sleep, friend. You've been on the go for nearly twenty-four hours. You won't be able to think about your next move clearly while you're out on your feet."

He was right, of course. Every bone in my body ached. I took a taxi down to Irving Place and let myself into my apartment. I just about had enough juice left to check for messages on my phone answering service. There were none. I noticed as I fumbled my way out of my clothes that it was a little after five in the morning. I must have slept almost before I stretched out on the bed.

The bedside phone woke me. I didn't want any part of it. The sun was streaming through the windows. I hadn't thought to pull the curtains when I turned in.

The phone rang and rang. I finally looked at the

bedside clock, eight-thirty. I'd had about three and a half hours sleep. It wasn't nearly enough. I finally picked up the phone. I guess I didn't sound friendly.

"Sam Tyler here, Peter."

"Sam, I've only been in the sack about three hours," I said. "Can you call back about lunch time?"

"I think you should know, Peter," he said. "Marilyn has disappeared."

It didn't make sense. I said so.

"She slipped away sometime in the night," Tyler said. "Took her car. Left no messages for anyone. Do you have any idea where Capra is?"

"I know where he was six or seven hours ago. I was with him. A private club called the Golden Bough out on the Island."

"Could Marilyn find that out?"

I felt a cold finger run along my spine. "He wasn't making any secret of it," I said. "In fact, he was being quite public about it. It provided him with a sort of alibi."

"Peter, we've got to stop her before she gets to him," Tyler said.

"I'm a guest out there," I said. "I can be there in a little more than an hour."

"I hope that's soon enough," Tyler said.

I put down the phone and lay there on the bed, trying to pull myself together. Then I sat bolt upright. I'd been too foggy to remember that my phone might be tapped. If it was, then Capra would be ready for Marilyn—and for me!

2

One of the experiences that has repeated itself many times in my life as a man and as a reporter is the unexpected happening, the pure chance, that changes a whole course of events.

I was in a hell of a hurry to get dressed and take off for the Golden Bough, ahead of Marilyn who had murder on her mind. I had phoned my garage to have my car ready and I literally charged out of the apartment, nearly knocking down a girl who was standing outside my door, about to reach for the bell. Beth Ryan grabbed my arms to keep from falling.

"The Dallas Cowboys could use us!" she said.

"Are you all right?"

"I'll let you know in a while," she said. "I told you I'd be in touch this morning. Did you know I live just around the corner from you? I went out for some breakfast and thought I'd just try ringing your doorbell."

I told her, quickly, about Tyler's call and that I was on my way to the Golden Bough in the hope of forestalling Marilyn's hysterical intention.

"Oh, God, I thought she'd wait at least until after the funeral," Beth said.

"Her kind of rage doesn't wait. I know."

"I'll walk you to your car," Beth said.

She looked very nice that morning, dark hair hanging loose down to her shoulders, a simple summer print dress accenting her elegant figure. She had an easy, swinging walk that kept pace with me without any difficulty. She told me she'd spent a good part of the night going through J. W.'s notes and transcribed tapes.

"He has so much inconsequential stuff on Capra, on Jefferson Fry, on the Vickers Creek sheriff. Most of it doesn't make much sense to me—yet," she told me. "I guess J. W. hadn't been able to make it add up."

"He wanted it to come up Capra, but it never did."

"J. W.'s material is like the pieces of a jigsaw puzzle," she said. "You move it around and move it around, hoping you'll find two pieces that fit together. Like Thelma Reeves."

"Who is Thelma Reeves?"

"I take it you don't buy lingerie for ladies," Beth said, smiling at me.

"Not lately," I said.

"Thelma Reeves operates a fancy boutique up on Madison Avenue," Beth said. "All the ladies who spend big bucks for clothes go there. But she got famous first as a soap opera queen. She played Angela on "Secret Corridors"; ten years' worth I'd guess. Beautiful woman."

I stopped by my car. The garage people had brought it out to the curb. "What does a soap opera actress have to do with the price of eggs?" I asked Beth.

"Her name in J. W.'s file on Capra," Beth said. "No notes, no comments; just her name in Capra's file."

"Capra is said to have women stashed away all over the map," I said.

I suddenly didn't want to be alone. Beth could be loaded with bits of information that could lead to that "hole on the fence," if Marilyn Travers's madness would let me get around to it.

"Out at the Golden Bough they seem to be surprised that I don't have a gal in tow," I said. "Would you like to ride out with me? We could talk, and you might be very useful if we find Marilyn out there."

She gave me a wide smile. "Why Mr. Styles! Are you by any chance propositioning me?"

"If I were, would you go for it?"

She looked away. "Who knows?" she said. "Just now my whole world is turned upside down."

Top down, it was a wonderfully warm summer day, the kind of day in which, if you were interested in a lady, you'd drive her out into the country somewhere and hope for the best. I had an extra pair of sun glasses in the glove compartment and I gave them to her. She sat beside me, her head resting against the back of the seat, long legs stretched out. Traffic took most of my attention till we hit the expressway that would take us out to the Golden Bough.

"You say your life is turned upside down," I said, as we got rolling.

She didn't look at me. The sun reflected against the dark glasses, hiding her eyes. "I have had a perfect job, interesting, totally absorbing," she said. "I thought it would last forever. J. W., I was certain, would never die." A little shudder ran over her. I knew how she felt. J. W. had seemed as permanent as the Lincoln Memorial.

"Was there more between you and J. W. than a boss-secretary relationship?" I asked.

A faint smile moved her lips. "That's an impertinent question, Peter."

"I know. I thought it might help to talk about it."

"Once, a couple of years ago," she said, "J. W. took me to Mexico City where he was working on a case. We had some free time, a wait while something developed. A man and a woman working together, a tropical climate, a glamorous place. It—it just happened one night."

"And after that?"

"Nothing," she said, almost harshly. "J. W. was deeply in love with Marilyn. He and I never even discussed the possibility of making it a—a habit."

"Do you think Marilyn ever knew about it?" I asked.

"J. W. never kept anything from Marilyn," she said. "Not just his private life, but his work. She sat in on the preparation of his cases. He may have told her about that one time in Mexico. If he did, she never showed it to me in any way. If she knew, I think she'd have understood how it could have happened. I think she'd have been satisfied that it wasn't an affair, just a moment."

"But you loved him?"

"Of course I loved him. You can't work as closely as I did with a man and not love him. If he'd wanted me on a permanent basis I'd have said yes. But he didn't." She moved, restlessly. "I want to get Capra almost as badly as Marilyn does, Peter. Damn him!"

"J. W.'s way, legally, in the courts," I said.

"That may be too good for him," she said. She was silent for a moment. "What will happen to Marilyn if she manages to get to Capra?"

"Temporary insanity, if she manages to kill him," I said. "Hospital for the criminally insane. End of the line as far as living is concerned."

"I guess she thinks she's already at the end of the line," Beth said. She reached out and touched my hand on the steering wheel. "Thanks for being impertinent, Peter. It somehow seems to have helped to share my big secret with someone. Helps to keep it alive."

"A girl like you, there must be men in your life," I
She laughed. "More impertinence? Oh, there were—quite a few before I went to work for J. W. I was the newly emancipated female in the early seventies. 'Love 'em and leave 'em' was my notion. Then there was J. W. and I couldn't really love him the way I wanted and I couldn't leave him." Her fingers tightened on my hand. "Have you been watching in the rearview mirror, Peter?"

I glanced up. There was a string of traffic behind us.

"That black sedan with the New York plates," Beth said. "He's been behind us ever since we got on the expressway. Slows down when you do, speeds up when you do."

I tried him out by stepping down on the gas and swerving out around the car in front of me. Beth was right. The black sedan, a Chevrolet Impala, stayed with us.

About a hundred yards further on there was a rest area at the side of the road. I pulled off onto it without warning. The Impala swept past, the driver hunched over the wheel so that I couldn't get a real look at him.

"Capra covers the world," I said.

Ten miles further down the expressway Beth touched my arm. She was looking up into the rearview mirror. The Impala was behind us again.

Being tailed angered me but it didn't concern me. We were headed into "Capra country." He'd know where we were without spying as soon as we went through the iron gates outside the Golden Bough. As we stopped outside those gates I saw the Impala speed past us. We were about to be accounted for both outside and inside the grounds.

The man at the gate greeted me like an old friend, and tipped his hat to Beth in a semi-military salute. I thought he looked pleased that I'd found a woman for myself.

"Mr. Wainwright said you were expected back," the man said. "He's kept your rooms for you."

I drove the car to Crampton House. We had no luggage, but we went into the ground-floor rooms I'd been assigned. Beth, who had been staring goggle-eyed at the white buildings with their red tile roofs, looked around her, unbelieving.

"I haven't checked," I said, "but Frank Devery tells me the showers have gold faucets."

She walked into the bathroom to see for herself.

"Could be," she said, when she came back. "What *is* this place, Peter?"

"Private club for the very, very rich," I said. "I understand J. W. and Marilyn were guests here more than once."

She nodded slowly. "He defended Daniel Markham in a tax fraud case some years back," she said. "He said he and Marilyn were visiting the Markhams at the Golden Bough. I thought that was the name of Markham's private home—like Travers Hill."

"The world does turn in a strange way, doesn't it?" I said. "Daniel Markham was Stanley Capra's father-in-law. Mrs. Capra was Nancy Markham."

She stared at me. "So Marilyn knows this place, might even be welcomed here."

"Might be," I said.

My last conversation with Capra had involved his suggestion that we talk again this morning. It was only a few minutes after ten. It seemed like years ago when we'd made that date; it was only about eight hours.

I told Beth what I was headed for. I suggested to her that she have a look around outside. If Marilyn had come here, openly, her car with Massachusetts plates should be somewhere. I could hear Marilyn's cold voice. "I'm not going to shoot Stanley Capra from behind a tree while he's walking his dog in the park. I mean to confront him, let him know why he's going to die, and give him a moment of terror I'm going to enjoy for the rest of my life!" If she was here, and Capra didn't guess why, she'd be waiting for a moment when she could be alone with him, or at least in control of the situation.

"I'll find her if she's here," Beth said.

"Good girl," I said. "She's got to be stopped, even if I have to warn Capra."

"Peter!"

"I mean to get him legally, Beth. It's the only way any of us can survive this, live with ourselves."

The ever-present Wainwright greeted me in the reception hall.

"Glad to see you back, Mr. Styles. I understand you brought a companion with you." His smile might have been the smirk on the face of a small boy who has just told a dirty joke.

"I was to look up Mr. Capra again this morning," I said.

"He and Mrs. Capra are having a late breakfast in the main dining room," Wainwright said. "I'm sure they won't mind if you join them. Mr. Capra said you might be asking for him."

I wondered if the men in the Impala had some sort of radio contact with the people here. If my phone on Irving Place was tapped they'd have known I'd ordered my car. The man in the Impala could have been waiting near the garage for me. Beth and I just hadn't spotted him until we got out on the expressway.

The dining room was on the opposite side of the reception hall from the bar. It was a beautiful, sunny room, picture-windowed. Standing in the doorway I could hear the crash of the surf on the beach. There were a couple of dozen tables, only two of them occupied. Capra and his elegant-looking wife were at one and, some distance away, Ben Martin, the vice president in charge of dirty tricks, was buried in the financial pages of *The Wall Street Journal.*

Capra spotted me instantly and stood up, beckoning to me to join him.

"Welcome aboard, Styles," he said. "I don't believe you've met Mrs. Capra."

She was a handsome woman, I suppose about sixty. She spent money for even casual clothes, and for makeup that looked like no makeup at all. I thought Nancy Capra and Marilyn Travers could have come out of the same finishing school. Marilyn the strong, aggressive one; Nancy the gentle, submissive one. But both cut out of the same cookie mold.

"I've read so many of your pieces in *Newsview,* Mr. Styles," she said, "and liked them."

Capra gave me that bright smile of his. "You may not care for Mr. Styles's next feature, my dear. I think he thinks he can find some way to scalp me."

A polite smile from the lady who obviously didn't believe that anyone could touch her husband.

"Sit down, Styles," Capra said. "Coffee?"

A waiter had materialized from somewhere. I hadn't had any breakfast. Coffee would be welcome. I sat down at the round table facing the lady. A tiny frown creased her forehead.

"Ever since the dreadful news yesterday I've been deeply concerned for Marilyn Travers," Nancy Capra said. "Her whole family wiped out!"

"She's a very tough, very strong woman," I said. "Right now all that concerns her is finding out who's responsible." I glanced at Capra. "The time for grief, for sorrow, I think will come later."

"We were once quite good friends," Nancy Capra said. "Mr. Travers defended my father in some sort of tax suit. Marilyn and J. W. visited Stanley and me here at the Golden Bough on several occasions. I liked them both so very much. I wish there was some way I could help her."

I couldn't tell Nancy Capra that the best way to help Marilyn was to keep her away from that smiling bastard sitting next to her.

"Mr. Styles believes that the ogres of big business planted that bomb on J. W.'s plane," Capra said. "That's why he's here instead of back at Travers Hill, helping Marilyn to bear her tragedy."

"Oh, no!" Nancy Capra said.

"The reason I'm here this morning," I said, "is because Marilyn slipped away from Travers Hill some time during the night and no one there knows where she's gone. It occurred to me that she might come here."

"Why?" Capra asked, his smile gone.

"Because she knows we'd help her," Nancy Capra said.

"Or because she thinks Loring Industries may be responsible for what's happened to her," I said.

"Nonsense!" Capra said. His smile didn't come back. I think he knew what I was talking about without my spelling it out.

The waiter brought my coffee.

"There seems to be no end to ugliness," Nancy said. "I saw on television this morning that a young teacher from Vickers Creek came to a violent end on the Hotel Beaumont last night. Did he have any connection with Janet Colmer or J. W.?"

"J. W. was on the way to Boston to see him," I said.

"And I suppose you're dreaming that Loring Industries had him thrown out a window," Capra said.

"That was an early thought," I said. "But a friend of Hardesty's, a professor, has pretty well convinced the police that it was suicide. Hardesty had been deeply depressed for some time."

Capra let his breath out in a long sigh. "It's a relief to know they don't think Loring is responsible for all the violence in the world," he said.

That was how Maxvil wanted him to read it. I'd done my part. I think he also understood that if Marilyn showed up it wouldn't be to plead for sympathy. Better he should protect himself than let her run wild.

He pushed back his chair. "If you'll excuse us, Nancy, Mr. Styles and I have matters to discuss."

She stood up and held out her hand to me. "If you see Marilyn," she said, "please tell her I'm ready to do anything I can to be of help."

I took her hand and was shocked to feel how cold it was. We watched her cross the room, erect, almost graceful.

"She's very special," Capra said, and sounded as if he meant it. "She never forgets a good deed."

"The Markham case?" I asked.

His laugh was mirthless. "The damned old fool was guilty as hell, but J. W. got him off." He straightened his shoulders. "Well, Styles?"

"I think I've heard all you have to say," I said. "You were quite right last night when you said we had no proof of anything that can be used against you. But those of us who cared for J. W. are never going to stop looking for it."

"If you can fix the guilt for the bombing it won't lead to me, Styles, or to Loring Industries. I have to warn you, though, that, if while you're looking you suggest in print that I or my company have any connection with it, I'll slap a libel suit on *Newsview* that will put your little rag out of business."

"We have very smart libel lawyers who read all the copy," I said.

Watching him and his fixed smile I sensed what his weakness was. He had the capacity for an almost overpowering instant anger. He could be goaded, I thought, into a personal violence he would regret later. He could coolly plan a monstrous action like the bombing of J. W.'s plane, or have a man waiting to throw Hardesty out a fourteenth-story window. There'd be no evidence to involve him, no trail leading to him. But step on his foot in the elevator and you'd be liable to get a rib-crushing elbow in your gut. We might never get him for the crimes we were certain he'd masterminded, but he might be maneuvered into an impulsive action that would do him in. Fifty years ago the federal government was never able to get the Al Capones, the czars of the rum-running empires, for their crimes. But they went to jail, one by one, for income tax violations. Maxvil was right, I told myself. If we could find the "hole in the fence," we might get Capra for something else. What we got him for wasn't that important. Get him, put him out of circulation, and let him know who got him and why. That ought to be good enough for Marilyn and Beth and the rest of us who'd cared for J. W.

"Last night," Capra said, "I offered to answer any questions, show you any books or records. Unfortunately, I can't wait around for you to think up something to ask, or something you want to see. Nancy and I are leaving here in the next hour."

"Where can I reach you if I need to?" I asked.

He shook his head, still smiling at me, as though I was some sort of backward child. "I've been about as accomodating as you could expect of me, Styles. I've instructed Curtis Bond, my chief of staff, to listen to any requests you have to make. If he thinks supplying you with what you want will get you off my back, he'll give you the answers, or anything else, you want. If he has doubts, he'll know how to get in touch with me. I've been interested to meet you, but let me tell you that I have no wish to continue our acquaintance. You've let yourself be sold on an absurdity. There's no pleasure in listening to the same tune played over and over. So, if you'll excuse me—"

I watched him go, tall, strong, confident. He was going to be a hard man to bring down—unless, somehow, he could be caught off guard.

I found Beth sitting on a retaining wall that looked down over the beach and the rolling surf. She was still wearing my sunglasses.

"This place is hard to believe," she said. "Invite me here sometime for a month. It would take that long to try everything it offers."

"Any luck?" I asked her.

She shook her head. "I went through the parking lot, told the attendant I had left something in your car. Unfortunately, he remembered you hadn't parked it there. But I had a chance to look around pretty thoroughly. Marilyn's car is a grey Datsun sedan with Massachusetts plates. I didn't see it. I don't think it's there."

"She could have parked in front of one of the residence buildings, as we did."

"Unless there's some secret place off in the woods somewhere, I've pretty well covered the territory," Beth said. "I risked asking one of the stewards. Would you believe they're actually running around with trays of drinks at this time in the morning?"

"The rich have rich habits," I said. "Asked him what?"

"If he knew where I could find Mrs. Travers. He said he knew Mrs. Travers from several visits but he didn't believe she was at the Golden Bough now. Didn't seem at all curious that I should be asking for Marilyn."

"Capra's entourage is taking off," I said. "If Marilyn doesn't turn up in the next hour, she will have missed him. It'll be safe for us to leave, too."

"To what next?" Beth asked.

I sat down on the wall beside her. From there we could see Markham House, the residence building where the Capras were staying. Three cars had pulled up in front of the building and an army of bellboys were bringing out bags, golf clubs, a big picnic hamper, and storing them in the trunks of the cars.

I told Beth Maxvil's hole-in-the-fence theory. "I'd like to go over J. W.'s notes and tapes with you, see if we can come up with a lead he missed."

"Like Thelma Reeves. I don't know why she sticks in my gut, Peter. I guess it's just because she doesn't belong in the notes. Nothing about her. Just her name. J. W. never mentioned her to me."

"Here goes the king of the universe," I said.

Capra and his wife came out of Markham House, named after Nancy's father. Curtis Bond, the crew-cut chief of staff, was with them. There were four other men, unknown to me, in plain business suits. The Capras and Bond got into the lead car, driven by a uniformed chauffeur. The four other men split up, two in each of the other two cars. One of them led the way, followed by the Capras. The third car brought up the rear. The Capras were well protected.

"Marilyn has missed her chance here," I said. "Shall we go?"

"Capra doesn't take any chances, does he?" Beth said.

"Those four men have been waiters, bellboys, bartenders, while he was here," I said. "No way to get at Capra if you wanted to survive."

"Peter, take me to China," Beth said. "I'd feel better there, I think."

I had one thing on my mind as we drove away from the Golden Bough. I stopped at the first gas station we came to and used the telephone there. I called my private eye friend, Joe Steiger, told him I thought my phone at Irving Place was bugged and asked him to meet me there in forty-five minutes.

Steiger was there when Beth and I arrived. He is almost as wide as he is tall, a very fat man. He has colorless hair, streaked with grey, which he combs in little strings over a large bald spot. His mouth is flabby, rubbery, and there is always a little black cigarillo dangling between his lips, spilling ashes down the front of his silk shirt and gaudy tie. He has little black pig-eyes, penetrating as gimlets. He wears a white linen suit, summer and winter. I asked him about it once and he said he'd bought Sidney Greenstreet's wardrobe from Warner Brothers. He certainly patterned his image after the late character actor. He looks like a flamboyant, soft poseur, but he's one of the toughest guys in a tight corner, as I have reason to know.

He acknowledged my introductions to Beth with a courtly, old-world bow. He wheezes a little when he has to walk a few yards. We went into my apartment. From the pocket of his white coat he took a small leather case of tools, mostly used, I guessed, for picking locks. He had my phone apart in two minutes and held it out to us.

"Very nice, very sophisticated little piece of gadgetry," he said. He seemed to be interested in exhibiting his skills to Beth. He took the tap out and put the phone together again.

"Can you tell how long it's been there, Joe?" I asked him.

"Whoever put it in was an expert," he said. "No scratches, no marks."

"Does this mean there's someone in the basement, listening?" Beth asked.

He beamed at her. "I said 'sophisticated,' Miz Ryan. The listener can be blocks away, soaking in a hot tub. I would have told him what he could do with his gadget before I unhooked it if you hadn't been present." He turned away from Beth, almost reluctantly. He has a weakness for pretty women. "Anything else, Peter?"

There was a lot else. I asked Beth if she'd consider making us some coffee and eggs while I caught Steiger up on the main show. His kind of thinking was something I badly needed.

He sat in my big, overstuffed arm chair, chin drooping, eyes half-closed, ashes dribbling down his front. I knew he wasn't dozing. He listens relaxed. I took him from Vickers Creek to Bartram Airport and Travers Hill, to the Beaumont, to the Golden Bough. Before I'd finished, Beth came out of the kitchen with coffee and a how-would-you-like-your-eggs.

Steiger stretched, as though he'd been sleeping in a cramped position. He lit a fresh cigarillo, his heavy eyelids narrowed against the smoke.

"There are two places where I might be of some use to you," he said. "I may be able to locate Marilyn Travers for you and throw a few roadblocks in her way. I might be useful in Vickers Creek."

"My God, Joe, all you'd have to do is walk down the main street in Vickers Creek and the whole town will know who you are and why you're there. They do a quick run-down on strangers."

Steiger gave me his flabby smile. "It sometimes pays to advertise," he said. "The people who won't talk won't talk anyway. The people who might talk may take a chance if they know there is someone to listen." Ashes bounced off his shirt front as the little black cigar moved up and down between his lips as he talked. "The bombing of Travers's plane already has the local police, the FBI, federal aviation, and God knows who else working on it. Maxvil, a good man, has your window job at the Beaumont under control. I'd only muck things up by moving in on those two areas."

"First things first," I said. "Stopping Marilyn is my top priority. The other things can take their place in line. How will you go about finding her, Joe?"

Steiger rubbed his double chins with the back of his hand. "To make sure to stop her I must find out where Capra has gone. If she's as determined as you say, that's where she's headed."

"How can she locate him?"

"Same way you did," Steiger said. "Old haunts, old houses, old homes, old women; mutual friends who don't know she's carrying a gun in her purse."

"How will you find him?"

"Capra can't hide, he's too well known, Peter. He can protect himself, but he can't hide."

Beth came in from the kitchen with a tray loaded with juice, eggs and bacon, toast, a jar of honey. Steiger's eyes widened.

"Are you married, Miz Ryan?" he asked.

"Not just now," Beth said.

"What a terrible pity," Steiger said. "But I suppose that should give unattached males like Peter and me some hope." He sighed as he tucked a napkin she'd brought under his chins. "I'm afraid I'm going to have to wolf this down, Miz Ryan. Finding Marilyn Travers is not a matter that brooks delay."

He wasn't kidding. He shoveled in his breakfast almost before I got started and heaved himself up out of his chair. "Be in touch if you hear anything from Miz Travers, Peter," he said. He walked to the front door and picked up his white Panama straw hat from the table where he'd left it. He looked back at Beth. "Why do I always meet beautiful women when I'm busy?" he said, and went out.

Beth stared at the door that had closed behind him. "I've been undressed in public a number of times in my life," she said. "But your friend is a master. I feel naked!"

"Maybe, when you weigh three hundred pounds, you tend to dream," I said.

"As long as he just keeps it to dreams!" she said.

I found myself looking at her, doing a little vague dreaming myself. I should have known that you don't think about "sugar and spice and everything nice" when you're sitting on top of an erupting volcano. It was erupting again as I sat there, eating a delicious breakfast and looking at a very pretty girl who just might help put an end to bad dreams.

My phone rang—my free and clear and once-more-honest phone. It was Sam Tyler, still up in Bartram.

"All hell has broken loose here, Peter," he said. "Did you—have you seen Marilyn?"

"No. But she hadn't gotten to Capra as of a couple of hours ago. What's wrong?"

"The Colmers' cottage; you were there yesterday?"

"Yes. You know I was."

"Burned to the ground," Tyler said.

"Jerry Colmer?"

"That's the hell of it, Peter. I got him out on bail

yesterday afternoon. Someone died in that fire. They assume it was Jerry. There isn't much left for the local coroner to deal with. Two bullets embedded in the skull. They think he may have set fire to the house and killed himself. Captain Garner's calling it a confession."

"That Jerry set the bomb on J. W.'s plane?"

"Yes."

"And you think?" I asked.

"I don't believe it for a minute," Tyler said, his voice steadied. "He saw Janet and his kids about to board that plane. He'd never in this world have let them take off in it if he knew."

"Then how does it add up?"

"It can close the investigation," Tyler said. "Whoever really set that bomb can be off the hook as far as the authorities are concerned. They'd like the case closed. They don't want the murder of J. W. Travers and his family left unsolved. Someone saw a way to help themselves out of a mess."

"Smell like Capra to you?"

"As long as we keep going down that street, who else?" Tyler asked.

3

It was almost too much to take in. In just a little more than twenty-four hours a small holocaust had wiped out five members of one family plus two other people connected to them, Professor Hardesty and Steve Meadows, the pilot of the Beachcraft Baron. I hadn't even thought about Meadows. He was a spear-carrier, an extra, an "innocent bystander." Yet he had, in his innocence, triggered the disaster in the air. Did he have a girl, a wife, perhaps even children of his own? The massacre of people I cared for had kept me from asking questions about a stranger. There must be people somewhere who were closer to Virgil Hardesty than the phony Clark Forrester. Did Jerry Colmer have parents, brothers, sisters? Had he gathered up a girl for himself in the period of separation from Janet?

As I told Beth what Sam Tyler had reported, there was only one image that persisted: a smiling, unworried Stanley Capra, with a vast fortune and a powerful corporate army to protect him and cover for him. There were dead people, piled up like cordwood, eliminated to protect him from—what?

I tried to reach Maxvil on the phone, but could do no

better than to leave messages for him with his answering service and at his office. Frank Devery had already heard about Jerry Colmer. *Newsview* had a man in Bartram covering the plane disaster who had actually helped fight the fire at the Colmer cottage.

"Bobby Woods, bright kid," Devery told me. "I didn't want to call you at your apartment because of the possible phone tap."

I explained to him that it was clear now.

"No doubt the charred body in the cottage is Colmer's," Devery told me. "Bobby just phoned. Dental charts match up. They've found the handgun that killed him in the debris. It is Colmer's, licensed to him. The police are calling it arson and suicide. They are convinced it solves the bombing of Travers's plane. Embittered son-in-law planned a murder and accidently killed his own wife and kids. Couldn't take it. Case neatly closed."

"Until we prove otherwise," I said.

"I wish I thought that was as simple as you make it sound," Devery said. "Mass murder to cover the frame-up of Janet Colmer in Vickers Creek? It's too much, Peter, even for a cold-blooded sonofabitch like Capra."

"J. W. was on to something else," I said.

Devery made a growling sound. "You talk about seven murders, Peter. You're leaving out an eighth: Jefferson Fry. As sure as hell those Vickers Creek goons went to that motel to kill him. Janet, naked in his bed, was window dressing after the fact. We're back at square one, chum. The bombing of the plane and five deaths are now explained by Colmer's 'suicide.' Hardesty's dive out a window is explained as 'suicide.' The cops are going to walk away from the whole horror and Capra will have caviar and champagne for supper."

"Not Maxvil."

"He's got to have facts, whatever he may believe," Devery said. "Like I said, square one. What about Marilyn Travers?"

"Steiger's looking for her. If she can be found, he'll find her."

"And anytime Capra wants to reach out and stop you from pestering him, he'll know where to find you, Peter. I don't relish the thought of your becoming a dead hero."

"I've got to find something before I'm dangerous to him," I said.

"Capra can just get bored with you."

"I hope to keep him looking some other way," I said.

"That will be Columbus Day," Devery said.

Beth Ryan sat staring at her uneaten breakfast as I gave her the gist of Devery's thinking. She finally looked up at me, her eyes wide.

"Is it so important to you to carry on with this, Peter?" she asked.

"Yes," I said. "J. W. and the kids and Janet mattered to me. The others are all tied into it. Nobody can be allowed to get away with it."

"Who elected you to stop them?"

"I elected me," I said. "They were my friends. That makes it my business. It's a news story. That makes it my business."

She nodded, slowly. "I loved J. W.," she said. "I guess that makes it my business."

"Too dangerous," I said.

"If it's not too dangerous for you, it's not too dangerous for me," she said.

I had known another woman like this and lost her. I also knew that you couldn't argue at such a moment. I reached out and touched her hand. I was reminded of Nancy Capra. Her hand was so cold.

"You're a doll," I said. "You can be most useful by helping me sort out all the information J. W. had collected. As Devery said, we're back at square one. J. W. was killed for what he knew, or was on the verge of knowing."

"I wish to God I knew what it was, Peter. Nothing he said to me in the last weeks of working with him indicated to me that he was close. He hoped Virgil Hardesty knew something about Vickers Creek. He had no idea what it might be."

"Let's go over what he had, page by page, word by word," I said. "Maybe we can see something or hear something J. W. missed."

The bulk of J. W.'s files and tapes were in his office on Park Avenue. A few handwritten notes and two tapes he'd made the last days of his life she had brought down from Travers Hill after the disaster, not yet put together.

We piled everything on a long stretcher table in a kind of boardroom in the office. The newest things Beth read aloud to me, translating a kind of shorthand he used which she understood. Hardesty had called from Boston. He couldn't talk on the phone because he thought his instrument was bugged; he didn't trust J. W.'s phone at Travers Hill. That, too, could be tapped. J. W. had agreed to fly to Boston.

"J. W. didn't think his phone was tapped?" I asked Beth.

"It hadn't occurred to him," she said, "but he had Charles Shay, the houseman, and Al Bostick, his bodyguard, go over all the phones—the way Steiger did at your place. Took them apart. Nothing."

Square one, I told myself, was Vickers Creek. There was a mass of stuff on the town, the local sheriff and his deputies, a transcript of Janet's trial. There was also a file on Jefferson Fry, the black activist. J. W. had believed Janet, but he had wanted to know everything there was to know about Jefferson Fry.

I have to tell you it would have taken weeks to do what I had suggested to Beth; go over what he had, page by page, word by word. There was enough material for a three-volume history of the case.

There was something in the Fry file that attracted my attention. Jefferson Fry, it appeared, was a married man with five kids, ranging in age from ten to two. His wife, named Carmen, lived in an apartment in Harlem with the children. J. W. had gone there to see her. His notes were sort of half-sentences. "Carmen Fry, a beauty about thirty. . . . Kids, well-mannered, well behaved. . . . Doesn't believe her husband and Janet were having an affair. . . . Wouldn't have been the end of the world if they were. . . . He was away so much—'fighting the good fight'—he was a normal man with normal impulses. . . . Not trying to save me pain, she said, she just doesn't believe it. . . . Not in Vickers Creek—too dangerous. Froze up when I mentioned Capra and Loring Industries. . . . Jefferson took on too big a giant, was all she would say. . . . Feeling he'd talked to her about Capra, but she wouldn't open up. . . . Refused to appear at Janet's trial. . . . Nothing she could testify to that would help. . . . Frightened woman, I think."

Square one?

"I think I'll go see Carmen Fry," I said.

"I'll go with you," Beth said.

"You stay here and keep digging."

"I'm going with you," Beth said. "I might get more out of a frightened woman than you can, Peter."

There was an address for Carmen Fry in J. W.'s file,

and we took a taxi up into the black center of the city. We stopped in front of an old brownstone, its front steps and sidewalk cleaner than most other places in the neighborhood. Two children, a boy and a girl, were playing hopscotch on the sidewalk.

"Does Mrs. Fry live here?" I asked the boy.

"My mother's in the rear apartment on the first floor," the boy said. "Who shall I tell her wants to see her?"

I guess the kids were watched, because a handsome black woman appeared on the top step.

"What do you want with the children?" she asked.

"Mrs. Fry?"

"Yes."

"My name is Peter Styles. This is Miss Ryan who is—was—J. W. Travers's secretary."

"Oh my God!" Carmen Fry said.

"We'd like very much to talk to you, Mrs. Fry," I said.

"It's too late! It's too damn late!" she said.

"We have our wounds, too, Mrs. Fry," Beth said.

I don't know what Carmen Fry saw in Beth, or heard in her voice, but after an instant she relaxed.

"If you think it can possibly do anyone any good," she said, and stood aside for us to go into the house.

A dark hallway, a door standing open at the far end. We found ourselves in what I suppose was the living room, with clean windows overlooking backyards where garbage was stacked high and laundry flapped on lines. The room was comfortably furnished, with reproductions of American painters tacked around the walls. There was one section that contained shelves of books. A quick glance suggested that whoever had collected them was more interested in history and biographies of political figures than fiction.

There came an awkward moment.

Sitting in an oversized armchair facing the door we came through was a black man with wide, white-rimmed eyes fixed on us. It was a warm summer day, but this man had a heavy blanket pulled over his legs and his hands were under it, out of sight.

"This is Madison Fry, my husband's brother," Carmen Fry said from behind us.

The Fry men were named after presidents it seemed. I said, "Hello, Mr. Fry."

He didn't move. His eyes didn't seem to blink. He just stared. "Madison can't hear you," Carmen Fry said. Her voice was bitter. "He is a vegetable. Can't hear, can't speak, paralyzed from the neck down. Don't let it embarass you. He's past caring."

"How—?" I heard Beth say.

"We are a crime-cursed family, Miss Ryan," Carmen Fry said. "My husband was murdered. It would have been better for Madison if he'd suffered the same fate. He was the night watchman in a building on Madison Avenue. Thieves broke in and left him like this."

"How dreadful!" Beth said.

Carmen Fry turned to me. "I don't know what possible help I can be to you, Mr. Styles."

"May we sit down?"

She gestured toward a couch and a couple of chairs. She made no move to sit herself. She just stood facing us, hands locked behind her back. We sat, feeling uncomfortable. Madison Fry, the vegetable, stared and stared. I suddenly realized he wasn't looking at us, wasn't interested in us. Whatever went on inside him, he was looking inward.

"You've heard what happened to Mr. Travers and his family?" I asked.

"On the television," Carmen Fry said. "And all the

neighbors kindly came to tell me that the girl Jefferson was supposed to be involved with had been blown to pieces."

"You met J. W. Travers," I said. "He came here to see you when he was preparing for his daughter's trial."

"It wasn't the best of moments," she said. "They'd fired ten slugs into my husband's head and chest. He wasn't recognizable when they shipped his body back home."

"We think the same people responsible for that blew up J. W. Travers's plane," I said.

She didn't speak.

"The police now believe that J. W.'s estranged son-in-law set the bomb that blew up the plane," I said.

"That girl's husband?"

"Yes. He was arrested, set free, and then, apparently, committed suicide."

"The man at the Beaumont?" Carmen Fry asked.

"Also a suicide, they think."

Carmen Fry bared her white teeth. "If I had any laughter left in me I would laugh," she said.

"Why, Mrs. Fry?" Beth asked.

"Everything that's happened since the day Jeff went to Vickers Creek has been too convenient. Since before that, since the day Madison was beaten to death—you might as well call it death—in the cellar of the building where he worked."

"The connection between that and these other things?" I asked.

Carmen Fry drew her deep breath. She took her hands from behind her back and they were white from being locked together.

"I have five children, Jeff's children, to care for," she said. "I have to educate them. Jeff started it." She gestured toward the books. "If I could prove what I think, Mr. Styles, I would talk to you. I can't. If they knew that I'd given you some kind of lead, they would punish me—through the children."

"They?" I asked.

"That's what I daren't talk about, Mr. Styles. A reporter like you must have friends on the police force."

"I do," I said.

"Ask to see the records of the case that involves what happened to him," she said, nodding toward the hulk in the chair.

"What will they show us?" I asked.

"I don't know, Mr. Styles. You don't believe in suicides, it seems. Maybe you'll see something in those records that the police didn't see. Maybe, in view of what happened yesterday, you'll see something that wasn't there to see at the time. Jeff saw it. I think that's why he was killed."

"Not because he was agitating against the nuclear plant in Vickers Creek? Not because he was supposed to be sleeping with a white girl?"

"Not for either of those reasons," she said. "Not for resisting arrest. They knew they were going to kill him when they went to that motel room. The girl just provided them with the crayons to color a picture."

" 'They' again."

"Are you talking about Stanley Capra and Loring Industries?" I asked her.

"I'm not talking about anyone!" she said, her voice gone shrill. "I'm not talking! *I can't talk!*"

A "frightened woman" J. W. had written in his notes.

"I've said all I can, more than I should," Carmen Fry said.

You couldn't push her to tell us more. It would have been cruel. I stood up.

"When did this thing happen to Madison Fry?" I asked her.

"In November of last year," she said. "Eight months ago."

"Is there any hope for him?"

"Only the hope to die," she said. "We, my children and I, hope to live. That's why I can't be of more help to you, Mr. Styles."

We thanked her and walked out onto the street. The children had been joined by others. They were interested in the taxi which was still standing where we'd left it. We hadn't asked the driver to wait.

"Thought you might have trouble finding your way home," he said.

We were grateful. I gave him the Irving Place address. I really had no notion where we should be going. I felt Beth's cold hand slip into mine.

"Blindman's bluff," I said.

"She's so damned scared, Peter!"

"Maybe we should all be," I said.

Back at my apartment I made us drinks. It was about four then. I called Maxvil at his office and this time I got lucky.

"You've heard the bombing case is solved?" I asked him.

"I've heard," he said. He sounded angry. "I'm sitting here waiting to hear from Boston—other friends of Hardesty."

"Did you know that Jefferson Fry has a brother named Madison?"

"Washington, Adams, Jefferson, Madison, Monroe—

that's all I can remember from fifth grade," Maxvil said. "No, I didn't know."

"He was beaten up in a robbery on Madison Avenue somewhere last November," I said.

"Hold the fort," Maxvil said. "It wasn't my case. It wasn't a homicide."

"The man's a helpless vegetable," I said. "You have to wait for them to die before you get interested?"

"Robbery detail handled it," Maxvil said. "I remember because the man's name was Madison and it happened on Madison Avenue. As I recall it, a woman owns a building, runs a shop on the street level, has a fancy duplex apartment on the upper floors. Someone broke in, stole a lot of costume jewelry and other stuff, beat up the night watchman. I didn't remember the last name. You say he is Jefferson Fry's brother?"

"Name of the woman who owns the place?" I asked.

"Don't recall. I can look it up for you. Why?"

"Could the woman's name be Thelma Reeves?" I asked.

"Christ, Peter, hundreds of names go across my desk. I don't remember. It wasn't my case. What's this all about?"

"Check it for me, will you, Greg? It might be the first decent lead we've had. J. W.'s notes contain the name of a woman named Thelma Reeves who operates a boutique on Madison Avenue."

"I'll get back to you," Maxvil said.

He did in about fifteen minutes, a drink and a half later.

"Thelma Reeves is your woman, friend," he said. "What does it mean?"

"I don't know. J. W. had her name tucked away in his file on Capra. Could be a hole in the fence."

Beth looked at me when I put down the phone. "I knew it," she said. "I felt it in my bones."

We really didn't have a damn thing. There was a name, scribbled in among notes on Stanley Capra in J. W.'s files. No comments on that name; a retired soap opera actress who ran a boutique, a woman's specialty shop on Madison Avenue. Beth, just in the role of a woman shopper and perhaps a soap opera addict, had recognized the name Thelma Reeves. J. W. had never mentioned Thelma Reeves to his secretary; Beth hadn't known the lady's name was in the files till she skimmed through after yesterday.

Now a frightened black woman, a widow-by-murder, caring for five very young children and the relic of her husband's brother, had pointed, oh so timidly, so indirectly, to Thelma Reeves. She had suggested that her husband had been murdered in Vickers Creek because of something connected with the brutal beating of his brother. She must have hinted the same thing to J. W.

Like moving around the pieces of a jigsaw puzzle, I've said, hunting for matching pieces. So we had Madison Fry beaten into an inhuman hulk in a building where Thelma Reeves maintained a shop and a duplex apartment. We had Carmen Fry suggesting to us that Madison Fry's beating might lead us to answers about J. W.'s death. And we had Thelma Reeves's name in J. W.'s Capra file. We had to fool with those three pieces and try to make them fit. But where to begin?

"You used to cover nightlife, theaters, Broadway, nightclubs, for *Newsview,* Peter," Beth said. "You must know some actor or actress who knows Thelma Reeves. She played the lead in 'Secret Corridors' five days a week for ten years. You must know someone who's worked with her, knows her well."

Just around the corner from my apartment, facing Gramercy Park, is The Players. A hundred years ago it had been the home of Edwin Booth, the great actor of his time, whose unfortunate brother, John Wilkes Booth, assassinated President Lincoln. Edwin Booth gave his lovely home as a club for actors, writers, artists, men-of-the-theater. It is a city landmark, its beautiful interior decorated by the famous Stanford White. Giants of the theater have passed through its rooms for almost a hundred years. It was once a totally male sanctum, with ladies only invited once a year. Today, in a changing world, ladies are guests for cocktails and dinner, gathered in the upper hall which is dominated by John Sargent's famous portrait of Booth.

It was cocktail time and I took Beth around to the club, hoping to run into someone I knew who also knew Thelma Reeves. We had only just settled at a small table in the dining room, under a picture of Jimmy Cagney, when I spotted Perry Ives. Perry is one of Broadway's top musical comedy stars—dancer, singer, comedian. He is a gay, witty fellow, and I use the word *gay* in its present-day meaning. He knows everyone in the theater, all the scandals, all the dirt. I beckoned to him and he joined us.

"I want you to know," he said, "that I gave the *worst* performance of my career at yesterday's matinee, thanks to you, Peter."

"What did I have to do with your performance?"

He gave Beth a wry grimace. "I dropped in here for a bite of lunch—very light lunch; my custom on matinee days. The bloody place was in mourning! Peter Styles was dead. Oh, the pain of it! I was into my fourth double

Scotch when the word came that Peter Styles was *not* dead. I'm not good when I'm potted. I had no excuse since you insisted on being alive, dear boy." His smile faded and he was genuine for a moment. "How lucky and how ghastly for you, Peter."

"I need your help, Perry," I said. "I need to know what you may know about an actress named Thelma Reeves."

"An ex-actress," Perry said. "I'll have to sit down for that and it will cost you a double Scotch." He sat. I gave his order to a waiter. "Did you know that I was on Thelma's *magnum opus* for three years? I was murdered in 1978 and haven't stepped in front of a television camera from that day on. I was murdered for murdering Angela, so elegantly played by our Thelma for ten years. She was retiring and they had to get her out of the script some way. Oh, the goings-on in those soap opera scripts you wouldn't believe, my dears."

"She retired two years ago?"

"Runs a little shoppie," Perry said, "where she sells black lace panties and blown-up bras—larger than life size, you know—and costume jewelry and giddy scarfs and God knows what else. Not entirely tasteless, but it surely doesn't provide enough income to support the elegant duplex apartment she has above the store. I don't believe even Elizabeth Taylor could afford what Thelma has up there."

"She must have made a lot of money in ten years on 'Secret Corridors,' " Beth said.

"Money, money, money. It's all relative, love," Perry said. "You get paid for talent and skills in this world. Thelma was a good actress, better than most, paid handsomely. But I think our Thelma retired from the screen because she could be better paid for higher skills."

"Selling black lace panties?"

"Oh, really, Peter!" Perry reached for the drink the waiter brought him. "Perhaps we should say *taking off* black lace panties—if you see what I mean."

"She's being kept by someone?" Beth asked.

Perry grinned at her. "Twenty years ago you would have *whispered* that question, love."

"So today I ask it right out loud," Beth said.

Perry sipped his Scotch. "We're living in a changing world, my dears," he said. "Twenty years ago my predilections would have created a scandal. Today I admit I'm gay and nobody bats an eyelash. Twenty years ago men and women, unmarried, carried on in cautious secrecy. Today they live together openly, even have children out of wedlock."

"Making the point that—?" I said.

He grinned at me. "You were obviously going to ask me, dear Peter, who is keeping our Thelma. I don't know. I've been dying to know, but I can't hear a whisper anywhere. She's playing it with someone the old-fashioned way. Never appears in public with anyone, there's never a word of gossip about anyone. Strange metamorphosis."

"Meaning?"

"In the old days our Thelma slept with everyone in town. Made no bones about it, was quite open about it. Then, suddenly, she turns into a nun, running a little shoppie. Whoever the gentleman is, he must be paying a very high price for her exclusivity for her to give up what she must have enjoyed so much—taking on the field."

I realized Beth was going to ask Perry if he'd ever heard of Capra in connection with Thelma Reeves, and I reached out and closed my hand tightly over her wrist.

She gave me a startled look and leaned back in her chair. Perry didn't miss the exchange. He stabbed at me with an accusing finger.

"You know who it is!" he said. "You just *have* to tell me, Peter! I'll even pay for my own Scotch, and no man hath greater love—"

"Beth and I suspect who it may be, Perry," I said. "It wouldn't be safe for you to know till we're certain."

"*Safe* for me?"

"You couldn't keep a secret like that. Gossip about it once and the man we have in mind might see to it that you never gossip again."

"Oh, *my!*" Perry said.

"You can help just a little more, Perry," I said. "You worked with her for three years, you say; what is Thelma Reeves like as a person? Not gossip, friend. Your own observations of her as a person."

He frowned. "Hard worker, good actress," he said. "Not Maggie Smith or Rosemary Harris, but good. Ten years in front of the camera, five times a week, and she *really* knows that technique. Best I ever saw at that. Nice person. Thoughtful of other actors, especially young people without much experience."

"How old is she?" I asked.

"Thelma? Late thirties, forty, perhaps. Full of vitality. Sexy, God knows. I didn't believe when she quit 'Secret Corridors' that she was giving up acting. I just thought she was sick to death of Angela; that's the character she played. I always thought she hoped to make it big on Broadway or in Hollywood. After she quit the soap no one saw her for a few months. Well earned vacation, we thought. Then, suddenly, there is the little boutique on Madison Avenue, with our Thelma the nominal owner. I mean, she's not behind the counter, not seen there often.

Her name's on the shop, but I've stopped in a half dozen times and never found her there."

I wondered. "She exists, though?" I asked.

"Oh, she exists," Perry said. "Been seen at the theater, always sitting at the back, dark glasses. Millions of people would know her by sight. She was their beloved *Angela* for ten years. They'd want autographs if they recognized her. A few of the people who worked with her have tried harder than I to renew a friendship. She's changed, they say. Not the old outgoing Thelma; remote, not wanting old friends. Like Garbo, she apparently 'vants to be alone.' Sick of acting, she told one of them. Sick of being someone else every day of her life."

"And no obvious man in her life?"

"Not a whisper of one," Perry said. "Oh you bastard, Peter, you know who it is!"

"When it isn't a guess, Perry, I'll tell you," I said. "And thanks."

Beth and I walked out onto Gramercy Park. Twilight was setting in, a warm red light from a setting sun in the west.

"Let's go have a look at the shop," I said.

"It'll be closed," Beth said. "It's after six."

"I wasn't going to buy you a present, love," I said. "I'd just like to have a look at the neighborhood, places she may shop, eat."

We hailed a taxi. Beth knew the shop was in the Fifties and she directed our driver. We sat close together and I was aware that she'd linked her fingers in mine. There wasn't anything coy about it. She was watching the traffic as the driver worked his way west to Madison. She felt a need to be close and I was glad she did.

"Capra could afford to buy a human life," she said, unexpectedly.

"If there was a price on it," I said. "He can afford to buy anything on earth if it has a price."

"J. W. didn't have a price," she said. "Nobody even tried to buy him off. He'd have told me, I think."

"One of the things a man who lives in Capra's world knows without asking is whether an object, or a man, or a country is for sale. If it isn't he just takes, he doesn't ask."

"Or kills."

"Or kills," I said.

"Is there any way on earth to prove what we think, Peter?"

"Hole in the fence," I said. "We get him for something else—hopefully."

Thelma Reeves's boutique—it was called, of all things, "The Delight Shoppe"—was in a small, narrow six-story building wedged between two glass-and-steel office buildings. How it had escaped the real estate pattern of the area was a puzzle. We paid off the taxi. The entrance door to the shop had a shade pulled down over the glass top half, and there was an ironwork protective door locked on the outside of it. The entrance to the apartments above the shop was next to it, a small vestibule with the usual brass mail boxes and two nameplates: "Smith" and "Mariotti."

"I wonder which she is?" Beth asked.

"I bet on "Smith," I said. "People rarely use any imagination when they fake a name."

We walked around to look in the shop window. Perry Ives had been right. There were black panties and bras and batik scarves, a display of costume jewelry, plus Staffordshire dogs and other toy carved animals. There was a plastic girl with a painted face wearing an old-fashioned wedding gown and a lace veil.

"You come here," Beth said, "to buy that small little

exquisite something, not to outfit yourself." She looked around at the tall buildings. "This neighborhood is all business, Peter. She doesn't shop here or eat here."

There wasn't really anything we could do there. We couldn't barge in on Thelma Reeves without more amunition than we had. I should have suggested to Beth that I take her to her apartment and leave her to lead her own life. I didn't.

"Shall we go back to my place and check my message service?" I suggested. "I'll buy you dinner somewhere, if you'd like."

She smiled at me. "I'd like," she said.

It had been a long time since someone had shared a day with me like this. I realized how very much I had missed it.

We taxied back to Irving Place. My phone was ringing as I unlocked the front door. I hurried past Beth to answer it.

"Peter?" It was Joe Steiger's wheezing voice.

"You've found Marilyn?" I asked him.

"You were followed home," Steiger said.

"What are you talking about?"

"I haven't found Mrs. Travers," Steiger said, "but I found Capra. She hasn't; not yet."

"What did you mean I was 'followed home'?"

"I am staked out across the street from Ye Little Delight Shoppe—or whatever," Steiger said. "I'm staked out there because Capra is upstairs, visiting someone. He's been there for about two hours now. A couple of his men have been hanging around outside. Security troops, Peter."

"And?"

"I saw you and Miz Ryan arrive. The goons saw you, too. I couldn't signal to you or call to you without attracting attention to myself. When you left one of the goons followed you. A dozen other people had stopped to look in the shop window and no one was followed. So they knew you. If you've been a bad boy, Peter, watch your step."

"You know who Capra is visiting?" I asked.

"No. Two duplex apartments over that shop. I assume a woman."

"You assumed right," I said. "Her name is Thelma Reeves."

"So now he knows you know. That just might not be healthy, friend. Like I said, watch your step."

PART THREE

1

"Madison Fry was never able to testify," Maxvil told Beth and me. I had called him after Steiger had alerted us. He had already dug out the records on the robbery at the Delight Shoppe last November and agreed to stop by my place with them on his way home.

"It's a routine story," he told us. "Unfortunately, in this day and age, God help us, robbery and violence go hand in hand. A thief or thieves broke into the building that houses the Delight Shoppe on November eighth. The robbery detail doesn't know whether there were one or more because Madison Fry couldn't testify. They guess at the time. Madison Fry covered five or six buildings in the neighborhood, made regular rounds. He checked off his calls on a list he carried and that was on him when he was found. The last check-off on his list was a building about a block away at two A.M. So they think this happened about two ten, two fifteen. Fry wasn't found until the shop was opened by the lady who manages it at about eight forty-five."

"Thelma Reeves?"

Maxvil shook his head. "Thelma Reeves owns the shop,

lives in a duplex above it. Martha Gillis, the store manager, worked for her. Miss Gillis found the shop had been broken into from the basement, safe cracked, expensive costume jewelry and other gimmicks stolen. Not a huge haul, a few hundred dollars worth. Miss Gillis called the police. When they came they found no evidence of a forced entry at the street level so they went down to the basement. They found Madison Fry there, beaten unconscious. The basement entrance had not been forced. Madison Fry was rushed to the hospital. He never came out of it, was never able to speak a word, not even able to answer a question by blinking his eyes 'yes' or 'no.' He was like you describe him today, a vegetable."

"Was the stolen stuff ever recovered?" I asked.

"No," Maxvil said. "There are some other things about the case that may interest you, though. The building is owned by Rubicon Real Estate." He waited for some sort of response from me. I didn't have one. "Rubicon," he said, "is a real estate holding company. They own a dozen buildings here in the city and a couple of hundred more across the country. Big business. It surely won't surprise you to hear that Rubicon is a subsidiary company owned by Loring Industries."

"Oh, wow!" I heard Beth say.

Capra, in effect, owned the building. Capra was, right now, spending time there with someone, presumably Thelma Reeves. I suggested that.

"Thelma Reeves, or someone named Smith, or Mariotti," Beth said.

"Miss Isabel Smith, who occupies the duplex on the second and third floors, is Thelma Reeves," Maxvil said. "No secret about it. Well-known actress, retired. She uses the name 'Smith' on her doorbell to keep autograph hunters and other fans from invading her privacy."

"Where was she when the robbery took place?" I asked.

"In her apartment, alone, she says," Maxvil told us. "Heard nothing. She wouldn't. The fancy apartment is insulated, soundproofed. The basement could have been in China as far as hearing anything down there was concerned."

"What about someone named Mariotti who lives above her?" I asked.

Maxvil gave me a grim little smile. "Anthony Mariotti, the only other tenant in the building, works, by the sheerest coincidence, for Loring Industries. He's a computer operator. He was in Baltimore, on a business trip, the night of the robbery."

"Checked out?" I asked.

Maxvil nodded. "Checked out."

"So what do we have?" I asked, impatient. "Capra owns the building; Capra, we assume, owns Thelma Reeves. He has been visiting her there for several hours right now. Madison Fry was destroyed trying to protect Capra's property. Carmen Fry thinks her husband, Jefferson, may have been murdered because of something connected with all this."

"You don't have a good part of that," Maxvil said. "Capra does own the building. But you only assume he owns Thelma Reeves. You only assume he's visiting her now. Ask him and he'll tell you he was having a business conference with his computer expert, Anthony Mariotti. Can your friend Steiger prove otherwise? And your Carmen Fry only thinks there is some connection between this and her husband's murder in Vickers Creek. There's a lot of assuming and thinking to get around, Peter."

"God damn it, Greg, where there's smoke—!"

"I play games with cases all my life," Maxvil said. "I'm

always juggling 'assumes' and 'thinkings.' My job is to turn them into facts."

"That's your job now," Beth said.

"Your job, young lady, should be to stay out of this," Maxvil said. "Peter's too, but he won't." He looked at me. "There are some things you should be asking, you know."

"Such as?"

"Such as, was there any sign of a struggle in the basement? A man was beaten into a senseless, helpless hulk there."

"Well?"

"There was no sign of a struggle. Nothing out of place except a locking bar on the inside of the cellar door. That was used to beat Madison Fry to a pulp, left behind, smeared with his blood."

"Fingerprints?"

"None. Robbery detail assumed—you see, we all do it—that the thief or thieves knew about Madison Fry's rounds, waited for him to let them into the building, and slugged him with the locking bar. Then they committed their robbery and left."

"What's wrong with that?"

"I told you, an *inside* locking bar. It should have been in place. Fry's job wasn't to go into the building, it was just to make certain that everything was locked. The door must have been open, at least unlocked, for Fry to go into the building. So someone was already inside. They didn't follow him in, they were already there."

"But you say the door wasn't forced," I said.

"Right." He waited a moment. "Oh, come on, Peter!"

"Assume," I said.

He grinned at me. "Okay, I assume somebody was already inside planning to go out that way. They had the door open, the locking bar off, when Fry walked in. He got his. No struggle."

"How did the thieves get in in the first place without forcing anything?" I asked. "Forcing, or picking a lock—whatever?"

"Because they were already legally in," Maxvil said. "Why would they go out by the cellar door instead of the apartment entrance? Because they had to carry something out."

"The loot," I suggested.

"What they took they could have stowed in their pockets," Maxvil said.

I stared at him for a moment. "You want to start over again?" I asked him.

"Just assuming, chum, just assuming," he said. "Someone in the building needed to carry something out, something they didn't want, couldn't afford, to be seen carrying. Not a pocketful of jewelry and knicknacks. They got what they were carrying down to the basement, unlocked the door from the inside, and in walks Madison Fry. They club him, may have thought they'd killed him. The poor bastard would have been lucky if they had. Still assuming, they couldn't carry him out as well as whatever they were already planning to take away with them. Fry will be found, so now they do a false robbery to cover their tracks, and take off with—the $64,000 question."

"You never bothered to 'assume' all this to the robbery detail?"

"God damn it, Peter, I only saw this report an hour ago! It wasn't my case."

There are tens of thousands of crimes committed in the city in the course of a year, from misdemeanors to felonies. The police are departmentalized. Robbery detail had no reason or obligation to share details of all their cases with homicide. If Madison Fry had died of his beating it would have been another story. Homicide, Maxvil told us, had been alerted by robbery when it appeared Madison Fry might die. The alert hadn't reached Maxvil in any detail.

"Someone made a joke about a man named Madison being beaten up on Madison Avenue," he told us. "Not seeing the detailed report, it sounded like an ordinary store robbery with an unfortunate violence added. There so often is. But this," and he brought his hand down on the report in front of him, "makes you wonder."

"Who slipped up?"

"Street cops answered the first call from Martha Gillis. They were primarily concerned with getting Madison Fry to the hospital. A detective from robbery detail probably came in somewhat later; just didn't pick up the fact that whoever attacked Madison Fry was already in the building, got there without forcing any doors or picking any locks."

"Could someone have hidden in the shop while it was still open?" Beth asked.

"And waited from six in the evening till two in the morning to walk out with a pocketful of almost nothing? I think not," Maxvil said.

"Maybe Capra doesn't want to be seen coming and going from the building, uses the basement to avoid being seen?" I suggested.

"And kills the night watchman to avoid being seen?" Maxvil said. "Because someone must have thought they *had* killed Madison Fry. No, I don't think so, Peter. He owns the building. He may own the lady, Thelma Reeves. He certainly owns, in a sense, Anthony Mariotti, his computer expert. Who would he be hiding from?"

"Someone on the street, who might be watching the apartment entrance?"

"All right, but he owns the building, it's operated by his people for his convenience. If he wants to use the basement as a way of coming and going, he would know the night watchman's routine. He would know that Madison Fry checked the building about two A.M. every morning. He would have left before that or after that if he didn't want to be seen."

"Maybe there was some kind of emergency," I said.

"Oh, brother! That you can count on," Maxvil said.

Beth and I had acted on impulse in going to have a look at the Delight Shoppe and, as a result, we had put ourselves behind the eight ball. Capra knew now that we had tied him in with the shop, the building. If that had been the hole in the fence I was looking for, we had warned him, and he would stuff it up, guard it, make it useless to us. We had, carelessly, made it next to impossible for us to penetrate whatever secret that building held. Capra was ready for us. It seemed he was always ready for me.

Maxvil was another matter. He suggested that robbery could get a court order to search the basement under the Delight Shoppe, ostensibly to make certain that security arrangements, locks and bolts, were in proper order; make certain that precautions against a repeat of the eight-month old robbery were in place.

"Crime statistics show that once robbed you're likely to be robbed again," Maxvil told us. "The same liquor stores get hit over and over; the same banks, in the rash of bank robberies we've been having, are hit again and again. The criminal repeats himself, because once robbed you can be robbed again. Our excuse for a court order."

"But in reality?"

"We'll look for God knows what," he said. "After eight months there's very little chance there's anything to look for. But it's worth a try."

"Anything that moves us anywhere is worth a try," I said.

Maxvil gave me a steady look. "You want advice?"

"Probably not," I said.

"I give it anyway. It's free. Get lost."

It's a slang phrase, "get lost." It's what the girl says to the boy who whistles at her on the street, what you say to the persistent magazine salesman. Maxvil, I thought, meant it quite literally. I waited for him to go on.

"You're hot, Peter," he said. "You were working with J. W. Travers, so Capra has you labeled 'enemy.' You turn up advising Jerome Colmer, talking to Hardesty, walking boldly into the Golden Bough, and finally looking over Thelma Reeves's boutique. You are getting to be not only a nuisance but a danger to him. You're going to be watched from here on in. Ten to one there's a man posted outside this building right now. You're not going to be able to go to the bathroom without Capra knowing it. If you get too close to something he must keep hidden, there'll be an accident."

"Surely you can protect Peter," Beth said.

"I can put him in jail, protective custody," Maxvil said. "Then after a few weeks, a few months, I let him out and he's behind the same eight ball. There's no end to this thing until, somehow, we put Capra out of business."

"My first priority is to keep Marilyn Travers from destroying herself," I said.

"You have Joe Steiger on that. You're not going to quit. I know that. But you can't function, Peter, unless you get lost—quite literally. You can't stay here, you'll be covered. You can't go to the *Newsview* offices, covered. You can't go to The Players, covered. You can't walk into Capra's world, covered. You can't be seen talking to Carmen Fry, covered. You can't go back to Travers Hill, covered."

"So what the hell can I do?"

"Get lost."

"How?"

"What was the old Chesterton gag in a Father Brown story? 'Where do you hide a leaf? In a forest.' The best place for a man to hide is in a city of ten million people."

"Wearing a Halloween mask?"

"Disappear. Stay where you are just one in a crowd."

"And do nothing!" I said, bitterly.

"There's still the hole in the fence to find," Maxvil said. "Once you shake Capra's people you can still look."

"What about Beth? They've got her linked to me now."

Maxvil looked at her. "You go about your normal business, Miss Ryan: clearing up J. W.'s affairs. It was logical for Peter to spend time with you. What is in J. W.'s files and records? That doesn't worry Capra. If there had been anything, J. W. would have used it long ago. Peter's been after you for information you haven't got. He drops you and disappears. You're not a danger to him, Capra will think, and actually you aren't."

"That slip of paper with Thelma Reeves's name on it," Beth said.

"Just the name. Without the name, Steiger followed Capra there. I think if you'll just go about your business, Miss Ryan, you'll be safe. I'll have someone watching you, just in case."

"How do I get lost?" I asked.

"I'll lose you, chum," Maxvil said.

It was a strange maneuver to plan. I was to abandon my home, my friends, my professional contacts, and stay "lost" for God knows how long. What do you take with you? You have to have money—and a toothbrush, a clean shirt. How will you be least conspicuous: in a three-piece vested suit, slacks and a sports shirt and no jacket at all, work clothes that would suit a plumber or an electrician or a cab driver?

Maxvil could arrange to get money for me, even though we were past all bank closings. A couple of hundred bucks should do. I finally selected blue jeans and a turtlenecked seaman's shirt I had tucked away. These things, plus a toothbrush, razor, some clean underwear, and another shirt went into a brown paper bag.

It was time for Beth to take off. She came across the room to me, put her arms around me, and kissed me in what wasn't a sisterly fashion.

"Peter, dear Peter, please take care," she said.

I didn't want her to go. I didn't, somehow, feel she was safe. But she went.

Maxvil's plan was simple. He would take me, quite openly, to police headquarters. There I would change into the "get lost" clothes. He would provide me with money and I would then be spirited away in a police van to some other part of town, and—get lost.

While I was changing my clothes in his office, Maxvil ushered a man into the room. He was tall, dark, bearded, wearing shabby clothes. He was introduced as Sergeant Pat Cooper, an undercover cop.

"Pat knows of a rooming house on the West Side where he thinks you can shack in," Maxvil said.

"An old broad named Mrs. Waterson runs the place. She won't ask questions," Cooper said. "Tell her Pat sent you. Just Pat."

"We'll take you to within a block or so of Mrs. Waterson's in a police work truck," Maxvil said. "There'll be other men in the truck and you'll go out with them and slip away. Pat will go ahead of the van, make sure it isn't covered. If we've fouled up, he'll know and pass you the word."

"How do I get in touch with you?" I asked.

"Public phone booth. There are thousands of them. Capra can't have them all bugged, you know." He touched the instrument on his desk. "If this one is bugged, God save us all!"

The police work van was in an underground garage. There were already a half a dozen men in it when Maxvil took me there.

"Good luck," Maxvil said. "If you have the slightest reason to think you've been spotted and are being followed, be in touch."

"Will do."

"Maybe I ought to have my head examined for turning you loose, but I know you, Peter."

"There are eight people dead, murdered," I said.

"Do your best to keep it at eight," Maxvil said.

There was no conversation in the truck as we headed toward the West Side. The cops—I assumed they were cops—didn't seem to have any particular interest in me. We sat on side benches facing each other, four on one side, three on the other. The truck didn't ride like a Rolls Royce as it bounced through a pothole here and there. A man across from me leaned forward.

"We're staging a drug raid on a small bar and grill," he said. "Go in with us. The customers will all race for the exits. Mingle with 'em and take off."

It was as simple as that. We stopped across the street from a crummy-looking joint. The cops got out of the truck and moved quietly toward the entrance. I went with them, acting the way they did. Suddenly they charged through the front entrance, announcing a police raid.

There were perhaps twenty-five customers in the place and they all attempted to leave in a body. There was a side entrance, and I followed the characters headed that way. I saw the man who'd given me my instructions watching, and he nodded at me.

I was out on the street; people seemed to evaporate. I found myself walking west toward the address Pat Cooper had given me.

I hesitated outside a dilapidated-looking old brownstone. I spotted a figure standing in the shadows not far away. I wondered if we had failed before we'd even started. The figure emerged and I recognized Sergeant Cooper. He made a circle with his thumb and forefinger, an all-clear sign.

Mrs. Waterson, who answered a noisy doorbell, was right out of an old horror movie: aged, bony, wearing a filthy flannel bathrobe, and sporting a rather healthy mustache on a wide upper lip.

"I was told I might get a room here," I said.

She looked at me and my brown paper bag without approval.

"Pat sent me," I said.

"Pat who?" She sounded as though she was gargling.

"I don't know his last name," I said. "Just Pat," Cooper had said.

"If you had I'd know it was no 'Pat' I know," she said. "Buck and a half a night, in advance."

I paid her.

The room at the end of the downstairs hall was not to

be believed. There was an iron bed, rumpled bedclothes suggesting that someone had used them before me; a washstand with a cracked china basin and pitcher; one straight-backed chair. Two bare electric light bulbs in a wall fixture.

"Toilet down the hall to your left," Mrs. Waterson said. "You want a bath, the door's locked and it's an extra quarter. You have to ask me."

She left and I saw that the door didn't lock. I sat down on the edge of the protesting bed. I was lost, and I didn't like it.

It is extraordinary how dependent you are on things you may not necessarily be using. I didn't have any reason to call anyone on the telephone, but not having one at hand drove me up the wall. I wanted to call Devery, I wanted to call Maxvil, I wanted to call Beth to see if she was all right, I wanted to call Sam Tyler at Travers Hill to see if there was any news of Marilyn. I felt like I imagine a pregnant woman must feel when she wants a dill pickle in the middle of the night.

Finally I couldn't stand it. I walked out of my room and down the hall toward the front door. Mrs. Waterson popped out of the last door on the right. She was drinking beer from a bottle.

"Something wrong? You don't like the room?" she asked.

"It's only about ten o'clock," I said. "I thought I'd go out on the town for a little."

"Don't ring when you come back" she said. "I'll be asleep. Just walk in."

The glassed-in phone booth on the corner was like a magnet. If I used it I had to make sense. It wasn't enough just to make contact with a friend for company. I told myself I didn't know enough about Thelma Reeves. She, her little shop, the violence there eight months ago, were the keys to something.

I went into the phone booth and called The Players. I asked if Perry Ives was still there. After a wait while they paged him, he came on.

"I couldn't come in to see you, Perry," I said. "I'm in something of a jam."

"Dear boy!" he said.

"Perry, you told me that Thelma Reeves played the field before she retired two years ago. Was there someone at the top of the list, a number one?"

"I suppose Rex Callison was her most popular guy in those days," he said. "Some of us thought they might even be thinking of making it legal."

"But they broke up?"

"I suppose. She quit the soap. I murdered her, remember?" he laughed.

"Rex Callison, was he an actor?"

"A good one," Perry said. "Strange about him, Peter. Thelma retired. About a year after that Rex disappeared."

"How do you mean?"

"Just that. He dropped out of sight. He had a good part in a Broadway show. Didn't show up one night, understudy went on for him. He just disappeared. Nobody knows where or why. His agent, Dick Otis, called in the cops. Missing persons, you know? They never came up with a clue. Good career, good everything, popular, women. He just vanished."

"When was this?"

"Oh, last fall sometime."

I felt the small hairs rising on the back of my neck. "Could it have been in November."

"I suppose. Dick Otis would know. The cops would know."

"Tell me, Perry, did Callison see anything of Thelma after she retired?"

"I wouldn't know that, dear boy. That was their private business."

"This agent, Dick Otis you say, does he operate here in New York?"

"He has an office here in New York. Paramount building, I think. He's gotten me a couple of jobs in the past. I don't know where he lives. Could be here, or in the suburbs I suppose. What interests you about Callison?"

"He could tell me things about Thelma Reeves that you can't," I said.

"Well, Rexie boy just dropped out of sight, Peter. If missing persons couldn't find him I'd say you didn't have too much chance."

"Thanks anyway," I said.

I went to the Manhattan phone directory that hung by a chain inside the booth. Richard Otis was listed twice, office at 1501 Broadway, residence on Central Park West. I thought about it for a moment and then I called Maxvil at his home.

"Lonely already?" he asked me.

"Your Sergeant Cooper should be had for cruelty to animals," I said. "That place he sent me to!"

"It's supposed to be the kind of place Capra wouldn't expect to find you."

"It is that. Tell me, Greg, have you ever heard of an actor named Rex Callison?"

"Sure," he said, promptly. "Among the missing. Big todo at the time. Popular guy, good job, just disappeared. Missing persons had it for a while. No luck. Why?"

"Did you know he was Thelma Reeves's boyfriend before she retired?"

"I seem to remember a lot of women were questioned about him. I don't have the case file here, Peter."

"Callison disappeared last fall," I said. "It could have been in November. It could have been November eighth, the day Madison Fry got his."

"Assuming again?"

"Maybe just a coincidence," I said. "Greg, I want to talk to Callison's agent, a man named Otis. How do I pass myself off as a cop?"

Maxvil laughed. "People do it all the time. You look a bit too honest."

"I have a hunch about this, Greg. It could be important."

"What's your name?"

"What are you talking about?"

"Your cop name," he said. Peter—Peters? Say you work undercover for homicide. I'll back you up if they want to check. Undercover cops don't carry badges. No chance this Otis character will know you by sight? You use to work the Broadway beat."

"I'd like to chance it."

"I'll have the Callison file for you when you want it," Maxvil said.

A woman answered the phone when I dialed Richard Otis's home phone. I asked for him and a moment later he came on.

"My name is Peters," I told him. "I'm a police officer. I've come up with something on the Callison case and I'd like to talk to you."

"Jesus, yes!" he said. "You know where he is?"

"I'm about twenty minutes away from you," I said. "Is it too late for me to come up tonight?"

"Hell, no," he said. "You know something about Rex, I can't wait."

I had to announce myself from the lobby of the luxurious building where Richard Otis lived. The security man in that lobby didn't like my looks. I simply told him I was Mr. Peters and that I had an appointment with Otis. I didn't suggest to him that I was a cop.

Otis greeted me at the door of his apartment, waiting just outside in the hall for me when I got off the elevator. He was a pleasant, cheerful-looking man in his early forties, I guessed, fair-haired with a kind of Jimmy Carter smile. If he was surprised by my casual clothes he didn't register it, nor did he ask me for any kind of identification.

He led me into a handsome living room, the walls decorated with dozens of autographed pictures of famous people in show business. He introduced "Officer Peters" to his attractive-looking blond wife.

"We can't wait to hear what you have to tell us, Officer," Otis said. "But I can wait long enough to make you a drink."

"I'll pass, thank you," I said.

"So you've come up with something?"

"I'm afraid not what you hope for," I said. "But you may help me to get there. Do you recall the exact date that Callison dropped out of sight?"

"I'm not likely to forget," he said. "It was last November ninth. He was in *Lonely Boy,* a hit play. He left the theater after the performance on the night of the eighth, everything apparently okay. That was it. He didn't show up the next night. Missing persons never found any friends who'd seen him after the performance on the eighth. He was just gone. But you must know all that from the police records."

"Just checking your memory of it," I said.

Mrs. Otis was sipping a gin and tonic. "We've been over this dozens of times with the police," she said.

"Tell me what you know about Callison's relationship with Thelma Reeves," I said.

"Oh, brother!" Otis said. He reached for a cigarette in the pocket of his shirt. "Rex and Thelma were a hot item for a long time. It broke up when she retired."

"How did Callison take it—the breakup?"

"Badly. He loved the woman, I think," Otis said.

"We held his hand, night after night, for weeks," Mrs. Otis said.

"He was a friend as well as a client," Otis said.

"Was Thelma Reeves a client of yours?"

"Yes," Otis said, "in the early days. She'd left me before she quit."

"You know why she retired when she was at the top of the professional hill?" I asked.

"I know what she said. She was sick of it all, being somebody else day after day, week after week. She said she was ready to throw up from being Angela in 'Secret Corridors.' "

"But that isn't why," Mrs. Otis said, in a flat voice.

I waited for her to go on, but it was Otis who picked up the ball. "Money, a man," he said.

"Who is he, do you know?" I asked.

"No idea," Otis said. "She disappeared from the show-business scene almost as completely as Rex did later. Oh, she's around. No secret about where she lives. But she's dropped all her friends, shut herself away from everyone who knew her and was fond of her."

"Did Callison know there was a new man in her life?"

"Of course he knew," Mrs. Otis said. Thelma Reeves was not one of her favorite people. "There were always men in her life."

"But he didn't know who the new one was," Otis said. "She never appeared in public with anyone. He used to hang around that crazy shop she bought and runs, but he was never able to tag anyone. Whoever the man is he keeps himself pretty well covered."

"Rex thought this man must have some kind of hold on her to keep her locked up, shut away, out of her profession. One of the last times I saw him he said he was still trying to find out who the guy was. 'And when I do I may kill the sonofabitch!' he said."

"But he never found out?"

"If he did he kept it a secret," Otis said. "So what is it you have that's new, officer?"

"Maybe he did find out," I said, "and the sonofabitch killed him instead of the other way around."

I suddenly believed what I was telling him. Capra at work again.

"I've wondered about that, I can't tell you how many times," Mrs. Otis said. "Rex was hurt and angry. Thelma had really hooked him for the first time in his life. He was willing to marry her, that's how badly he was hooked. But he wasn't a romantic. He wouldn't just fade away, walk out into the ocean like the guy in *A Star is Born*. He would, I'd have bet, licked his wounds and found himself a new chick once he was convinced Thelma had definitely sold herself out of his world. I've often wondered if he caught up with Thelma's new guy that night and was taken out. I suggested it to the cops at the time."

"They never came up with a trace of him," Otis said. "Sooner or later a body turns up, doesn't it?"

"There must have been thousands that haven't," I said.

"It wasn't as though Rex had planned to go somewhere. No clothes gone from his apartment. He kept an engagement pad by his phone." Otis said. "Lunch date for the next day, dinner that night, lunch again the day after that. Never called any of those people to cancel out. Boom, gone, down a manhole!"

"The night Rex Callison walked away from the theater and disappeared something else happened," I said. "Thelma Reeves's shop was robbed."

"Was it that same night?" Otis asked. "I remember hearing about it. It must have been days afterwards. I, people in my office, were all too concerned about Rex to pay much attention to anything else. Is there a connection, Mr. Peters?"

"You can begin with almost nothing," I said. "Two people once in love, separated now for over a year; start with that. On November eighth the man disappears and the woman is subjected to violence."

"Thelma was hurt in that robbery?" Otis asked.

"No, but the night watchman whose job it was to check several buildings in the neighborhood was badly beaten. Eight months later he sees nothing, hears nothing, can't speak; a blob, a zero."

"How awful!" Mrs. Otis said.

"He's never been able to tell anyone what happened that night," I said. "If Rex Callison was still scouting around after months to find out who Thelma Reeves's boyfriend is, that watchman could have seen him. There's something I don't understand, Mr. Otis. How can a relationship between Thelma and a man be kept a secret for two years from what must be hundreds of friends, all curious about her leaving her career? Gossip, questions, must have been endless. How could she have an affair with a man for two years and his identify never surface?"

Otis shrugged. "My guess has always been that it's the man who has the other apartment in the building. His comings and goings wouldn't seem to be connected with her. Once in the building, she can go to his place, he to hers, nobody would know. There are no other tenants. It could be like living in one big house together."

"There must be cleaning people, maids, a building superintendent," I said.

Mrs. Otis laughed. "Don't think people haven't buzzed around them, offering modest, maybe even immodest bribes to find out who the guy is. Nobody's got lucky. No one works there in the evening, which I guess is the traditional time for lovemaking." She glanced at her husband. "Dick and I have never thought there was a 'best time' for lovemaking. Whenever you feel like it—which could be anytime. Apparently with Thelma it's after dark, after the help has gone home."

"The guy upstairs works," Otis said. "He's some kind of a computer expert. He can't run home in the middle of the day just to satisfy the curious."

"Dick's been making book on that guy," Mrs. Otis said. "One day Flora Sheffield, a client of Dick's, was in the shop. Thelma isn't often there, but she was that afternoon. In walks the guy from upstairs. Not bad looking, according to Flora. He tips his hat to Thelma and says, 'Good afternoon, Miss Smith.' Smith is the name Thelma has on her mailbox. She says, 'How are you, Mr. Makeloski'—or whatever."

"Mariotti," I said.

"They acted like the most casual acquaintances, people who pass in the front hall," Mrs. Otis said. "Flora wrote him off."

"It would be awfully convenient if he's it," Otis said.

"But why keep it so secret?" I asked. "Thelma, I understand, was never secret about her men before this."

"I ran into her once on the street," Otis said. "I asked her that, straight out. Who is the new guy? She told me, with gestures, what I could do with my curiosity."

"Mr. Peters is right. It's out of character," Mrs. Otis said. "She hasn't even invited a friend in for a drink in two years. She always used to like being with people. They flocked around her, encouraged by her. Suddenly she changes completely, becomes a recluse."

There wasn't any more to learn from the Otises. I thanked them for telling me what they had and promised to keep them posted if there was anything new on Rex Callison.

I walked down Central Park West to Columbus Circle. The city lights were bright. I was full of 'maybes.' I had no doubts about the identity of Thelma Reeves's lover, the man who kept her in luxury and in total seclusion. Stanley Capra was probably still there with her, Steiger waiting across the street for him to show. His comings and goings to that apartment over the Delight Shoppe must be covered so well. There had been two men watching the territory for him when Beth and I had gone to look in the shop window. They would scout out the area before he went in and before he came out. His wife? He'd always have a business excuse for being absent from home. I wondered about Thelma. Capra traveled all over the world, his wife with him a great part of the time. Did Thelma trail along behind, or was she left alone in her apartment for long absences? Like a sailor, with women in every port, Devery had said. Was he likely to transport a mistress on the back of a plane, or on another deck of a ship? He had women wherever he was going. If Thelma was left alone for those long absences, why did she stay shut away? 'Out of character,' Mrs. Otis had said. A woman who'd enjoyed many men now had only one who left her alone for weeks at a time. She apparently took no advantage of that, had no man or men who played second fiddle in her life. Why not? Love? Love of a man, of his money, of his power? She had to know that, if he chose to have her watched around the clock, she would be watched. If he chose to, he would know what she did with every hour of her day.

I wondered if she enjoyed just being herself instead of being Angela in "Secret Corridors."

I walked down Eighth Avenue, past the old Madison Square Garden site. Mrs. Waterson's hutch was only a block or so further down and another block west. I was back in my thinking to Rex Callison.

There he was, a popular actor in a hit show. He walks out of the theater after an evening performance and is gone forever; for eight months anyway. He hadn't, it seemed, in a period of some sixteen months before that night of November eighth, resigned himself to losing Thelma. He must have tried all kinds of ways to get in touch with her: telephone, letters, hanging around the Delight Shoppe waiting for her to show. She must have turned him off cold and hard when they did meet, and they surely must have met, not socially but on the street or in the shop. If I was right, Capra would know about this, know just how Thelma handled it. If seeing Callison was against the rules, she wouldn't even have had a cup of coffee with him.

I wondered if Callison had finally decided to get to Thelma, insist on talking to her, insist on being allowed to plead his case, no matter what the obstacles. Could he have found his way into the apartment section of the building, bombarded the door of the Smith apartment? Finally admitted, he could have found himself face to face with one of the most powerful men in the world. It would be a shock, I suppose, like walking in and finding your girl in the arms of the president of the United States.

Capra had his way of dealing with that kind of situation; he could buy what he wanted. I had to think he had bought Thelma Reeves. What about Callison? "Just go away, boy, and I'll buy you a tropical island, a harem of beautiful women, anything your little heart desires—except Thelma!" If the numbers got large enough, fantastic enough, Callison could have been had—or could he? I hadn't really found out enough about him from Dick Otis to make that judgment.

I paused for a few seconds outside the grim facade of Mrs. Waterson's rooming house. I was wondering if every man *does* have his price. I walked into the house and down the hall. I opened the door to my room which didn't look locked, and stepped in, fumbling for the light switch. I never got to it.

Another kind of light exploded in my head. I thought there must be two of them, clubbing at me, probably with gun butts. I remember opening my mouth to shout for help and hearing nothing.

2

I felt as if someone was ringing a gong inside my head. A bright light shone in my eyes, so bright I had to close them the moment I opened them.

"He's blinkin' his eyes," a croaking voice said. Mrs. Waterson!

I tried again and looked up into the bearded face of Pat Cooper, Maxvil's man. His lower lip was bleeding and he was blotting at it with a handkerchief. I turned my head to one side and saw that I was lying on the rumpled bed in the room Mrs. Waterson had assigned to me.

"Better get you out of here," Sergeant Cooper said. "Hospital a couple of blocks away. You got lumps like eggs on your head, plus some pretty nasty looking cuts."

"What happened?" I asked him.

He turned to the old woman. "Want to wet this towel again, Mom?" he asked. He took a towel off my head and handed it to her.

Grumbling, Mrs. Waterson went off down the hall with the towel.

"I'm just 'Pat' to her," Cooper said. "She doesn't know

I'm a cop. Wouldn't have anything to do with me if she knew."

I tried to push myself up on an elbow and I thought my head was going to split open.

"What happened?" I asked again, lying back.

"Followed you uptown, and back," Cooper said.

"Why?"

"Maxvil's orders."

"All you had to do was tell me and I'd let you know where I was going," I said. Followed by Maxvil's man, obviously caught up with by Capra's boys, I would have been angry if I hadn't hurt all over.

"It seemed stupid for you not to know," Cooper said. "Like you said, you could tell me where you were going and it would make things simple. When you got back here and came in the house I followed you in to tell you. Damn good thing I did. Two guys were all over you. No lights, no chance to see them. I waded in and they took off."

"We muffed it somewhere along the way," I said.

"How do you mean?"

"They knew where to find me, were waiting for me."

"You think Capra's people?"

"Who else?"

He took the handkerchief away from his mouth and looked at the bloodstains on it. "This is a pretty crummy neighborhood," he said, "pretty crummy establishment. When you went out, some of the goons hanging around decided to see if you had anything worth stealing. New tenant. I'm damn certain we weren't followed here from police headquarters, and I don't think you were followed on your trip uptown and back."

"Except by you."

"My job," he said. "You're not a permanent assignment,

you understand. I was to make sure you hadn't been spotted. I'm pretty damn sure you hadn't. Just bad luck you walked in here before they got away with your clean shirt!" He lifted a finger to his lips. "Old lady coming back."

Mrs. Waterson came back with a wet towel. It felt good when Cooper put it on my head again.

"You didn't see anyone hanging around here, Mom, who doesn't belong?" Cooper asked my landlady.

"I'd of kicked them out on their butts if I saw any strangers snooping in my house," she said.

"Well, I'm going to take my friend here to the emergency room at St. George's," Cooper said. "He might have a concussion or something."

"You gonna want to keep this room, pal?" Mrs. Waterson asked me.

"I think I better change locations," I said.

"No refund!" she said in a shrill voice.

"I didn't expect one," I said.

Cooper helped me up off the bed. I felt so dizzy for a moment I thought I was going to pass out again, but soon the world leveled off. We walked down the hall and out onto the street, I leaning heavily on Cooper's arm.

"You think you can walk a couple of blocks?" he asked. "Try to get a cab or an ambulance and the whole damn neighborhood will be gawking."

"I can try," I said. The truth is that just then I didn't give a damn whether school kept or not. It could have been petty thieves waiting for me in that room, or it could have been Capra's people. Either way they'd done a pretty good job on me.

The emergency rooms at St. George's were crowded and noisy. People were moaning and wailing and crying out. Night is a time for violence in the city—knife fights, muggings, God knows what. A businesslike young doctor took a look at my head and put in for a tetanus shot and X-rays. I got the shot and was wheelchaired to an X-ray room. Still in the wheelchair, I was pushed out into a sort of waiting room while the X-rays were developed.

I was suddenly overwhelmed by sleep. I'd had three and a half hours in the last thirty-six. A Puerto Rican woman, not far away, was praying, rhythmically, for a son who'd had his gut ripped open in some kind of brawl. That rhythmic praying was like a lullaby. My chin sank forward on my chest and I drifted away.

I don't know how much later it was that I opened my eyes and found myself looking at Greg Maxvil who was sitting in a chair facing me, smoking one of his perpetual cigarettes. He gave me a tight smile. I realized that while I'd slept I'd been wheeled into a small private office of some sort.

"You may hurt, but you're all in one piece," Maxvil said.

"I suppose I should think I'm lucky," I said.

"Care to catch me up? What the hell were you doing, perambulating around town?"

"Thelma Reeves is a kind of obsession with me, I guess," I said. I told him about my conversation with Perry Ives, the Rex Callison story, and what I'd been able to add to it from my visit to Dick Otis and his wife.

"So the music goes round and round and you think it comes out Capra," Maxvil said.

"That, too, may be an obsession," I said.

"Maybe not," he said. "You didn't get a look at the two guys who attacked you in your room?"

"No. It was pitch dark. They were waiting for me, Greg. If they were thieves going through my stuff, which was in one foolish paper bag, the light would have been on. I hadn't really reached for the light switch when they started clobbering me. There's no use trying to hide. Capra has a magic way of knowing where I am."

"Maybe you're right. So we take you back to your own bed where you'll sleep well, have a couple of cops openly covering you. While you get yourself slept out, I'll go over missing persons' file on Rex Callison. Maybe there's a lead in it."

"If I have to walk around under Capra's microscope, I can't just twiddle my thumbs, Greg. It's a question of whether he gets me before I get him."

Maxvil put out his cigarette in a saucer on the table beside him. "All of a sudden," he said.

"Meaning?"

"You've been involved in this thing for three or four months, beginning with Vickers Creek. Covering a news story, you start collaborating with J. W. Travers. Nobody pays the slightest attention. Travers hadn't, as far as you know, come up with anything vital—except news that Virgil Hardesty, a Vickers Creek boy, might have something. Well, he damn well must have. A bomb that silences Travers, a phony suicide that silences Hardesty, a chance to close out the bombing that silences Jerome Colmer. But you, famous reporter, walk into the lion's den at the Golden Bough. Everybody's all smiles, answers for your questions, offers of help. Be my guest, old buddy. Then you are seen looking in the window of Thelma Reeves's shop and you are an instant target."

"You've left out one step, Greg," I said. "I went to see Carmen Fry, and wound up looking in Thelma Reeves's shop window. J. W. went to see Carmen and wound up with Thelma's name in his file. Now a popular and successful actor walks offstage and disappears, and that leads us to Thelma Reeves again. Isn't all that enough to justify turning a little heat on the lady?"

"Let's try to keep the heat off you till you get caught up on some rest," Maxvil said. "You're no good to us or yourself, walking around in a fog."

When you're hurting it's awfully easy to let yourself be persuaded to stay out of the action. "Fog" very accurately described the state of my mind. It was a little after midnight when Maxvil got me back to Irving Place. A cop was stationed just inside the French windows that open onto my little garden, another in the hallway outside my front door, two more in a patrol car covering the street outside.

"I must be an important guy," I remembered muttering to Maxvil, who oversaw the arrangements himself.

"Important to me alive, important to Capra dead," he said.

My own place seemed like heaven after Mrs. Waterson's. I remember unstrapping my artificial right leg and foot. Wear it for as long as I had without relief and it begins to ache. I remember hopping, one legged, into the bathroom and standing under a steaming hot shower for a moment or two. Then I found my bed and felt myself dropping down into a deep, dark, blessed oblivion.

I slept right round the clock. It was afternoon when I woke with the summer sunshine streaming through the windows of my bedroom. After a moment or two to get oriented, I sat up on the edge of the bed, strapped my aluminum prop into place, put on a bathrobe, and walked out into the living room. A cop in plain clothes I hadn't seen before was sitting by the open French windows.

"We changed shifts while you were sleeping, Mr. Styles," he said. "I'm patrolman Zabriskie."
"Hi," I said.
"A few messages for you," he said.
I remembered we'd turned off the bedside phone. It had a jack attachment and you could just pull it out from the wall to cut it off. Zabriskie went over to the living room phone and picked up a pad.
"Mr. Devery called and said to let you sleep it out. Call him when you can. Someone named Steiger called and said *not* to let you sleep. I told him I had my orders. He raised hell with me but finally said to tell you there was no sign of the lady. A Miss Ryan called; call her at the Travers office. A Mr. Tyler called. He's in Bartram, Massachusetts."
I was feeling my head, gingerly. There were some sore spots, but nothing sensational. "That all?" I asked Zabriskie.
"The lieutenant," he said. "When you come to."
"I'm going to make some coffee," I said. "You want some?"
"Great."
I got the Mr. Coffee machine working and went back in the living room to the phone. Maxvil first, I decided. He wasn't at his office, had left no word where he could be reached.
Devery sounded concerned. He'd gotten the saga of the night before from Maxvil.
"Shouldn't you see your own doctor?" he asked. "Those creeps in the emergency rooms only care if you're alive."
"Well, I'm alive," I said. "Twelve hours sleep. Anything new?"
"Nothing you didn't know or suspect," he said. "The

cops and the FBI have closed out the bombing of Travers's plane. They've elected Colmer. They may be trying to trace where he bought the materials to make the bomb, but he's 'it' in their books."

"How nice for someone," I said.

"In Boston we haven't found any friends of Hardesty who knew he was depressed or suicidal. Only Forrester."

"Who will settle down in the south of France on Capra's dough," I said.

"We had a man on the Callison case eight months ago," Devery said. "Disappearance of a popular actor was a news story. He may have been grieving over Thelma Reeves, but he wasn't living without women. One in particular, an actress named Donna Simms. She insisted at the time there'd been an accident, a violence of some sort. He was, she said, happy with her, no problems. Missing persons never found a trace of any accident, not in New York, not anywhere. Puff of smoke, gone. One thing the night he disappeared."

"What?"

"Like most actors, he had a message service. That night, November eighth, he called in after the performance to see if there was anything for him. Operator remembers, I suppose because of what happened later."

"And was there a message?"

"They don't keep the messages after they're delivered to the client. If they did they'd have bales of them. The operator who took his call that night thinks there was a message, just a telephone number for Callison to call. She doesn't, not unnaturally after eight months, remember the number. It could mean something or nothing, Peter. Someone calls him, leaves a number. He calls back, doesn't call back, and vanishes."

"You know how to locate Donna Simms?" I asked.

"She's on the same soap opera Thelma Reeves used to be on—'Secret Corridors.' In the phone book, probably has a message service like all those people."

"Pumped dry long ago by missing persons," I said. "What about Thelma Reeves? They must have talked to her back then."

"Zero," Devery said. "Our reporter talked to her, too. Yes, she'd been close to Callison, but it had broken up some sixteen months before that night of November eighth. She'd seen him, casually, on the street a couple of times, but no real contact with him. It was all over between them. She had no idea if he had a new girl, what his life pattern was. They were, now, strangers."

"Probably has no connection with all the rest of this," I said. "And yet, and yet, and yet—"

"Hunch?"

"That keeps eating at me, Frank. My getting interested in Thelma Reeves apparently matters to Capra. So anything that relates to her, even the disappearance of a discarded lover, makes for hunches."

"Steiger get back to you? Let you know when Capra left Thelma's building?"

"He called while I was asleep. His message indicates he hasn't caught up with Marilyn Travers. He'll call again, I hope."

Just in case, I dialed Steiger's number. No answer after about eight rings. I hadn't expected to find him at home.

Maybe Sam Tyler, up in Bartram, knew something. He didn't. He had called me to find out if I knew anything. No word from Marilyn. She had left no kind of instructions for funeral arrangements or services. Sam was puzzled about what to do.

"Join the club," I told him.

The coffee was done and I poured mugs for Zabriskie and me. I began to think I was going to survive. I settled down by the phone again and called Beth Ryan at J. W.'s office.

"Peter! You're all right?"

"What made you call here?" I asked her. "I was supposed to be lost out in the city somewhere."

"Lieutenant Maxvil was thoughtful enough to call and tell me what had happened to you. Peter, I think someone followed me from my apartment here to the office."

"Probably a cop," I said. "Like you say, Maxvil is a thoughtful gent."

"I don't think it was a cop, Peter. It was someone I saw out at the Golden Bough."

"Have you told Maxvil?"

"I haven't been able to reach him," Beth said.

She was linked to me in Capra's book; seen with me at the Golden Bough, at the Delight Shoppe. I didn't like it. I realized, quite unexpectedly, that she mattered to me.

"Everyone I know who can help seems to be lost for the moment," I said. "Maxvil, my private eye friend Steiger—both out of touch. I'll find a way to get someone to you."

"Couldn't I come to you, Peter? There's no one here in the office but me. It—it's a little spooky."

"I'm not a very safe guy to be around," I said. "I have the feeling Capra's made up his mind about me. You stay where you are, love. I'll get someone to you."

I hadn't really thought it through until that moment. The attack on me at Mrs. Waterson's had to mean Capra wasn't waiting for me to get any more dangerous to him than I already was. How dangerous was that? I didn't have a thing on him yet except hunches. It had to be that

I was moving close to something hot, and the only direction in which I'd been moving was Thelma Reeves. It didn't make sense for me to just sit around, play sitting duck, and wait to be taken. Your best defense, my old football coach used to tell us, is a vigorous attack. If Thelma Reeves held the key to this chain of unthinkable violence, the chances are Capra would spirit her away to the other side of the world if we waited too long to get to her. It was that. or make sure we didn't move her way.

"Do you have instructions about me?" I asked Patrolman Zabriskie.

"Just to stick with you till I'm relieved," he said.

"I'm free to leave here?"

"With company," Zabriskie said.

"Keep trying to get Maxvil while I get dressed," I said.

I had made up my mind. I was going to get to Thelma Reeves and talk to her while I was still in one piece. Broad daylight with a cop to guard me seemed like as good a chance as I was likely to have.

I shaved, dressed, and from my handkerchief drawer I took a small police special I was licensed to carry. Perhaps I was a fool to try it without consulting Maxvil, but I had convinced myself that to wait any time at all might mean missing the boat altogether. It might already be too late. They'd had a good fourteen hours to get Thelma Reeves out of reach, if that was their plan.

Zabriskie hadn't reached Maxvil by the time I was ready. I didn't alert Devery. I knew he'd try to talk me out of it, and failing that he'd try to get in my way, stop me somehow. I could have used Steiger, but he still wasn't at his phone. I did leave word at Maxvil's office that I was on my way to visit Thelma Reeves.

I gave Zabriskie as much of the score as I could as we rode uptown in a taxi.

"If the lady doesn't want to talk to you, what can you do about it?" he asked.

"Play it by ear," I said.

"I can't help you break in, you know?"

"I know."

"Just keep me covered from behind," I said. "I don't want to get it in the back."

"You should wait for the lieutenant, Mr. Styles."

"I know, but where the hell is he?"

I'm not a movie star who's easily recognized on the street, but Capra's people would know me. I'd put on a pair of tinted glasses and I wore a hat, which was unusual for me in summertime. Madison Avenue was jammed with traffic, and we moved slowly.

"The lady may be in her shop," Zabriskie said.

"I don't think so," I said. "I think today she's going to stay undercover, if she hasn't already been taken somewhere."

We got out of the cab about a block away from the Delight Shoppe. We turned west on the side street where the entrance to the apartments was located. There was just a small vestibule with the brass mailboxes and nameplates—"Smith" and "Mariotti." There was, I saw, a third buzzer that was marked "superintendant."

"She isn't going to answer her bell if she doesn't want to see anyone," Zambriskie said.

I tried anyway, holding my finger on the "Smith" button for quite a while. There was no answer on the intercom, no click at the door lock. Mariotti didn't answer, he was probably at work.

"You know how to pick a lock?" I asked Zabriskie.

"I know how but I'm not about to," he said.

I tried the superintendant's bell. I suppose I stood there for four or five minutes with my finger on the button. I could hear a bell ringing on the inside. I was just about to give up when I saw, through the glass top of the door, someone approaching.

"Okay, okay, I'm coming," an angry voice said.

A man in blue denim work clothes opened the door.

"What the hell do you want?" he asked.

"I've been trying to rouse Miss Smith," I said.

"If she doesn't answer she doesn't want to see you," he said. He started to turn away and stopped. I looked back at Zabriskie. He was giving me the only help he could. Out of his pocket he'd taken his leather folder with his police badge in it. He didn't say a word, but he was holding it up for the superintendant to see. I took a cue.

"I'm a friend of Miss Smith," I said. "I have reason to think there may be something the matter upstairs. Take us up. If she's all right, that's that."

The superintendant hesitated, looked at Zabriskie, and shrugged. "One flight up," he said.

We climbed the stairs to what was the front door of the Smith duplex. The superintendant rang the doorbell. Nothing happened.

"You got a key?" I asked the super.

"Of course I've got a key," he said.

"Let's just make sure she's okay, and if she is, or isn't there—"

The super looked at Zabriskie's expressionless face. Nobody was going to say later that a cop had told the super to open the door. But the super thought that was what was happening. He unhooked a key ring from his belt, selected a key, and started to fit it in the lock.

The door was opened from the inside.

A woman with bright red hair, wearing a dark green housecoat, faced us.

"What's going on here, Spellman?" she asked the super.

"These gents said they thought something had happened to you, Miss Smith," the super said. "One of them is a cop. I don't know who this other joker is."

I played it straight. "My name is Peter Styles, Miss Reeves," I said.

It must have been a jolt. I saw a little nerve twitch along a high cheekbone. She must have been a beautiful young girl, and she was still a very handsome woman. But her face was frozen now. All the natural color seemed to fade as she stared at me. Her hands, at her sides, were clenched in two tight fists. She was making what must have been a big decision.

"It's all right, Spellman," she said. "Come in, gentlemen."

"I'll wait out in the hall," Zabriskie said.

I hoped he meant to keep the super busy and away from a phone that would alert someone.

I found myself in a luxuriously-furnished, high-ceilinged room. I am a bug on paintings, and I was aware, though I was concentrated on Thelma Reeves, that she was surrounded by a fortune in modern art. Only someone in Stanley Capra's financial brackets could have afforded paintings of this value to decorate an apartment. They belonged in museums.

"What can I do for you, Mr. Styles?" Thelma Reeves asked.

"You know who I am?"

She gave me a tight little smile. Her eyes were a brilliant grey-green—cat's eyes. Wary, cautious. "You wouldn't be in here if I didn't," she said. She gestured toward a side table. The current issue of *Newsview* was on top of a stack of magazines. "You seem to have been able to sell Spellman a bill of goods. Is your friend really a cop?"

"He's a cop. Assigned to protect me," I said.

"Why are you here, Mr. Styles?"

"Because I want to go on living," I said.

Again that little nerve twitched along her cheekbone. "Don't we all," she said. I wondered if those three words were meant to tell me what to expect from her? Nothing. Nothing because she, too, wanted to go on living.

She sat down in a handsomely upholstered armchair. She didn't suggest that I sit. I had the feeling that her long legs felt weak under her. She had to sit or reveal her anxiety. Slender fingers gripped the arms of the chair.

"We can talk frankly, Miss Reeves, or we can play games," I said.

"What do you want me to be frank about?"

"Stanley Capra," I said.

The cat eyes blinked. "Who is Stanley Capra?"

"Oh, come on, Miss Reeves," I said. "He owns this building. He provides you with this apartment and your store. He's been your lover for two years."

"So you know that," she said.

"Frankly, yes," I said.

"Frankly, I don't understand why that should be any of your business, Mr. Styles," she said.

"You must know about the bombing of J. W. Travers's plane two days ago," I said.

"And that you were a very lucky man," she said. "I also know that the police and the FBI have solved the case. A son-in-law, off his rocker."

"So they say."

"Would you mind getting to the point, Mr. Styles? The point being, why are you here?"

"So you are current with the news," I said, "which, being in the profession, I know rehashes the past with all that's fresh. J. W. Travers's history as a great defense counsel, the more recent events involving his daughter in Vickers Creek, the trial in which Travers attempted to link the shooting of a black radical named Jefferson Fry and his daughter's alleged involvement with Fry to Loring Industries. Some listeners might skip over that, Miss Reeves, but not you. Loring Industries is a dynasty run by your friend Stanley Capra."

"Yes, I know all that," she said. "I also know the courts cleared Mr. Capra and Loring Industries of any involvement in the Vickers Creek incident."

"And now the police and the FBI have cleared him of any involvement in the bombing of J. W. Travers's plane and the murder of five people. They have cleared him by accepting circumstantial evidence that Travers's son-in-law committed suicide which they believe was a kind of confession. They have cleared him of the murder of a man named Virgil Hardesty by calling that murder a suicide. That adds up to eight murders, Miss Reeves."

The knuckles of the fingers gripping the arms of her chair looked like white marble. "You have apparently flipped your wig, Mr. Styles," she said. She was having trouble with that treacherous little nerve in her cheek, but her voice was in perfect control. After all, she was an actress. "Are you imagining that Mr. Capra, who is, I admit, a warm and good friend, spends his time confessing murder to me? I suppose in your business you're entitled to wild speculations, but as wild as this?"

"Believe it or not, I hadn't imagined that Capra would confess any crimes to you," I said.

"Then why on earth this visit, Mr. Styles? I really

think I've had about enough of it, but I have to admit I'm dying of curiosity."

"Shall we talk about the eighth day of last November?" I suggested.

Shadowed eyelids flickered over the cat eyes. "I'm not likely to forget that day, Mr. Styles. My shop downstairs was robbed."

"Of a few hundred dollars worth of costume jewelry when there were thousands of dollars there, waiting to be scooped up."

"The thieves were evidently frightened off by the night watchman."

"I visited that night watchman yesterday," I said.

She jerked forward in her chair.

"Don't be scared, Miss Reeves," I said. "Madison Fry, your ex-night watchman, can't see, speak, hear, or feel anything. He was beaten into a human vegetable by the thieves who only took a pocketful of cheap jewelry from your shop."

"There was insurance that's taken care of him," she said.

"Insurance can't make him human again."

She brought one clenched fist down on the arm of her chair. "Please get to the point!" she almost shouted at me.

"That human vegetable turned me in your direction, Miss Reeves. Madison Fry was the brother of Jefferson Fry, who was shot by the Vickers Creek police, presumably when he resisted arrest. There are those of us who believe that Jefferson Fry guessed what really happened here that night of November eighth. That he went to Capra with it, threatened him with it. That Jefferson Fry wasn't shot because he was agitating against a nuclear plant in a small southern town, or because he was sexually involved with a white woman, but because he had something on your Mr. Capra."

She leaned back. "Really, Mr. Styles, what bullshit!" she said.

"I think not."

"Jefferson Fry had something on Stanley? What? That I'm Stanley's woman? We don't have a sign out over the shop, but it's not that dangerous a piece of information."

"I don't think it was that," I said.

I don't think she heard me. "It wouldn't have been necessary to kill Jefferson Fry to keep him from blabbing about me," she said. "There would have been simpler ways to keep him quiet."

"Money?"

"Of course."

"That's why I don't think that's what Jefferson Fry had on your man," I said.

"*What,* then?"

"Something else of some consequence to you happened on the night of November eighth," I said.

"I don't follow," she said.

"After his performance in *Lonely Boy* at the Alton Theater, Rex Callison walked out into the night and disappeared," I said.

She stared at me as if she didn't believe I'd said what I'd said. "What has Rex got to do with all this other nonsense?" she asked.

"You asked me to tell you why I'm here," I said. "It's to ask you that."

She shook her head from side to side. "I really think your brains are scrambled, Mr. Styles. Rex was part of my life for a number of years, but not last November eighth, and not for more than a year before last November eighth."

"Weren't you concerned when you heard he hadn't shown up the next night, November ninth, for a performance? Weren't you concerned when missing persons came here to ask you about him?"

"Of course I was concerned. You want frankness, Mr. Styles? For about six years Rex and I were, what people call today, roommates. We broke up. Things like that do break up, you know. I'd given Rex all I had to give. My life changed."

"Stanley Capra?"

"Yes, damn it, and if you print that in your stinking magazine, Mr. Styles, you'll be sued out of your socks. Stanley came into my life and I gave up my career because it pleased me to be available when he needed me and wanted me."

"But Rex Callison kept trying to get you back, didn't he?"

"Rex was a hard loser," she said. "I couldn't see him. I didn't want to under the circumstances. I didn't want anything to upset a perfect life I'd found for myself."

"This—and Capra?"

"This and Capra," she said. "Rex Callison had been out of my life for sixteen months the night thieves broke into my shop. He had nothing to do with the attack on the night watchman. Nothing that has ever happened here relates to Rex in any way."

"Where do you think he went? What do you think happened to him?"

"An accident!" she said. "Maybe some mugger on the streets who killed him and disposed of his body. This isn't a safe city, you know, Mr. Styles. Perhaps a suicide, a jump off a pier into the river, the tides took him out to sea."

"Let's not have another suicide, Miss Reeves," I said. "I'm already choking on two. Callison had found himself another girl, was apparently perfectly happy with her."

"Donna Simms?" She laughed. "Little Donna might not have been exactly what Rex was used to."

I don't know where it came from, but it surfaced. "The night Callison disappeared he checked with his message service after he left the theater. There was a message. A telephone number. Was it yours, Miss Reeves? Had you called him to tell him you wanted to see him?"

"You are really far gone, Mr. Styles," she said. "I keep telling you that, except for a couple of casual meetings on the street, I hadn't seen Rex for nearly sixteen months!"

"Had you had enough of Capra?" I asked her. "Did you want help to get out? Did Callison come here, and was he caught here by Capra or some of Capra's people? Mr. Mariotti upstairs? Does Mariotti spy on you, Miss Reeves? Is that one of his jobs for Loring Industries?"

A voice spoke from a far corner of the room, a familiar voice. "You did the best you could, my dear," Stanley Capra said. He was standing at the foot of the stairs that led to the second floor of the duplex. He must have been there all the time, heard every word we'd said. And he wasn't alone. Curtis Bond and Ben Martin, his two chief aides, were just behind him on the stairs.

Thelma Reeves had jumped up out of her chair at the sound of Capra's voice. Instinctively, I thought, she grabbed hold of me. Then her lips moved and she was whispering.

"*Please, for God's sake, help me!*"

Ben Martin pushed past Capra and came toward me. He was pointing an efficient-looking gun at me.

"Just keep your hands in sight, Styles."

"What happens if I don't?" I said. "Do I go out through the basement—like Callison?"

"Wise guy," he said.

He found my gun with the first pat of my jacket.

3

"It seems you are determined to become a classic pain in the neck, Styles," Capra said. He was smiling, that ever-present smile. He was almost unbelievable, this man. He moved with a kind of aristocratic grace; he wore an expensive tropical worsted suit with a certain style; the stage setting, this apartment where he kept a mistress, breathed elegance, taste, and staggering wealth without being in any way flamboyant. The paintings—a Matisse, a Renoir, a Chagall—had been selected by a man with an eye for beauty.

This man who found himself at ease with royalty, with the people who really rule the world, who helped guide the course of nations with his enormous power, was a cold-blooded murderer. He struck in a strange variety of places, from a motel room in Vickers Creek, to a private plane in the skies near Boston, to a luxury hotel in New York, to a cottage in the Berkshire hills, to Mrs. Waterson's filthy dive on the West Side. I was certain I had not been meant to survive that attack.

Now, as Ben Martin made certain that he had my only

weapon, I found myself believing there had been another murder done, perhaps in this very room. Evidence of that had resulted in the brutal destruction of Madison Fry in the basement of this building eight months ago.

And all the while I was hearing that strangled whisper from the chalk-faced Thelma Reeves, who had sunk back down in her chair. "*Please, for God sake, help me!*"

Zabriskie, my cop friend, was out in the hall, unaware that there was anyone else in the apartment than Thelma Reeves. Someone had said earlier that this duplex was soundproofed. Robbery detail had checked and accepted that as an adequate explanation of why Thelma Reeves had heard nothing on the night of the robbery and violence on the floors below on that November night eight months ago. There was very little hope of attracting Zabriskie's attention.

"You might just as well sit down, take the weight off your feet, Styles," Capra said. "You won't be going anywhere right away." He turned to the crew-cut Curtis Bond. "Check out, Curtis, please."

"The cop in the hall?" Bond said.

"We'll deal with him later," Capra said. "Right now the street climate interests me."

"Right."

Bond went out through a door at the rear of the room. I gathered there must be a rear way out of the building which would make it possible to avoid Zabriskie in the front hall—a service entrance, perhaps out through the basement where Madison Fry had met his particular disaster.

"Sit!" Martin said, holding his gun right under my chin.

Time was all I had to play for, not that time would matter too much in the long run.

"I think, Thelma, you should finish your packing," Capra said to the lady. "No great hurry, but when the right moment to go comes, we must be ready."

Thelma's wide cat eyes were fixed on me, as though pleading for me to say something, do something. What could I say or do? She stood up and walked, not too steadily, to the stairway that led to the second floor. Capra and Martin and I watched her go, as if it were a dramatic second act curtain. That whispered plea for help made me wonder if it was, in fact, a final curtain. She had known, all through her conversation with me, that Capra and Martin and Bond were listening. "You did the best you could," Capra had said to her—her best to steer me away, to convince me that there was nothing to my guesswork. Packing? Had it been their plan to get her away from questions, and had I been just a shade quicker than they'd expected?

"Sit!" Martin ordered again.

I was backed up against a sort of love seat and I just bent my knees and sat. Capra came close. He took his silver cigarette case out of his pocket and offered it to me.

"Smoke?"

"No, thanks," I said.

He lit one for himself. "God knows, I gave you every opportunity, Styles, to back off," he said. "I wonder if you would have done as much for anyone who was interfering with your life?"

"I don't have anything to hide," I said.

"I suspect your world isn't as complex as mine," Capra said. He took a deep drag on his cigarette and then put it out in an ash tray on the table next to my love seat. I had a feeling he was stalling, not quite decided on how to handle me.

"You asked Thelma quite a few interesting questions,"

he said, finally. "How did Rex Callison ever come into your thinking?"

"A loose end," I said. "Madison Fry pointed me here. Jefferson Fry, I think, guessed what had happened to his brother and why. Thelma Reeves's name appeared in J. W. Travers's file on you. Rex Callison disappeared into the blue on the same night that Madison Fry was beaten. Jefferson Fry is dead, Madison Fry is a vegetable, Callison is gone. They all fit together somehow, fit together here. I, you might say, wrote a script based on all that. I wanted to check it out for truth."

"Tell me how it reads," Capra said.

"I think Rex Callison came here the night of November eighth," I said. "I have no way of knowing whether it was an impulse of his own or whether your lady sent for him. One way or the other, I think he came here. I suspect you keep a close watch on Miss Reeves. Does Mariotti, upstairs, spy for you? I know there are men on the street. Someone alerted you, you came here, found Callison, and killed him."

"What horseshit!" Ben Martin said.

"No, let him go on, Ben," Capra said. His smile had a frozen look to it.

"Obviously Miss Reeves knows," I said. "She was here, she was present. You had to get rid of a dead man. I'm guessing you sent for help, if it wasn't already with you. Martin, here? Bond? It was the early hours of the morning, streets relatively deserted. Best way to carry out a dead man was through the basement under the shop. One of your people drove a car around to that basement entrance. You carried Callison down to the basement, took the locking bar off the door on the inside. Somebody, I suggest, went out to scout the street. Maybe you saw the night watchman coming down the block. That's when you made your first mistake."

"Oh?" Capra said.

"You didn't know, or you slipped up," I said. "Madison Fry's routine was just to check that basement door. If you'd put the locking bar back in place, he'd have found everything secure and gone on. Instead, he found the door unlocked, walked in, and got the full treatment from you or your people."

"Do we have to listen to this crap?" Martin said.

"We have time, Ben. We have lots of time," Capra said. "Do go on, Styles. I find your imagination quite fascinating."

"Second mistake. You didn't kill Madison Fry. You thought you had, I'm sure. You must have sweat a lot later when you heard that he wasn't dead. Would he talk? Would he tell what he'd seen? How long was it before you got the happy news that he would never talk?"

"There was nothing to talk about, except thieves he caught attempting to rob the shop," Martin said.

"Ah, yes, the thieves," I said. "You couldn't risk carrying two bodies out across the sidewalk and into a car. Someone had the bright idea of faking a robbery. Not much of a robbery to be sure, but it satisfied the police. You took Callison away and ditched him somewhere. Several months go by, and then Jefferson Fry approaches you in Vickers Creek. A dedicated radical, he wasn't so concerned with his brother's tragedy as he was with his cause. Close the nuclear plant in Vickers Creek or he would tell the police enough to start them investigating a murder. I imagine he was waiting for your answer when you had him killed."

Capra had moved away as I spun my little fancy. He

was standing, back to me, at a window which must look down on Madison Avenue. Whoever had engineered the soundproofing of this place had done quite a job. Hundreds of people were passing back and forth only a few yards, less than a football field away, and there wasn't a sound—not a taxi horn, not the rumble of a bus, nor the squeal of a tire on the pavement. There was an army out there that could help—if they knew someone needed help.

Capra spoke without turning away from the window. "You suggested to Thelma that, having murdered Callison—a crime you dreamed up and for which you haven't a shred of proof—that I went on killing and killing."

"Eight times and one miss," I said.

He turned from the window, a look of genuine surprise on his face. "A miss?"

"Me," I said. "Last night. The cop who was guarding me was just a shade too fast for your people. They didn't get the job finished."

He came back across the room and sat down on the arm of the chair that Thelma had vacated.

"You're a very interesting man, Styles," he said. "I have to tell you I think you're wasting your time working for a salary, however generous, at *Newsview*. Hollywood pays millions for your kind of inventive genius. Let me collaborate with you." His genial smile was back in place. "Our hero reporter faces sinister head of big corporation whose hands are bloody from a series of murders." He looked down at his hands and actually chuckled. "But our hero has a problem. He can't prove a damn thing! How does the phrase go? 'Murder most foul' has been done, but there is no way whatever to make any kind of charge stick. The sinister head of the big corporation—and the heads of big corporations are always sinister villains in the public mind—really has nothing to fear from our hero except libelous accusations. Now our hero has forced his way into the apartment of a lady who is very precious to the sinister villain, armed with a gun, no less! By chance, the sinister villain and two of his associates are in another room of the apartment. They disarm the hero, not knowing what his intentions are and not wanting to take risks. That, I think, brings us up to date, Styles. Now what does the sinister villain do next?"

"I suspect our hero goes the way of all men who interfere with the villain's bloody career," I said.

"With Ben here as a witness?" Capra said. "With Thelma and Curtis as witnesses?"

"Long since bought off—or frightened off," I said.

"Oh come, Styles, this has gone far enough," Capra said. "I don't anticipate with pleasure your making your fantasies public. I have the very human impulse of wanting to silence you. I think I've assessed you correctly and that there's no point in offering you any financial inducement. Am I right?"

"No point at all," I said.

"And so we will have a nasty washing of imaginary dirty linen in public. I regret it. I will take every possible legal action to make you pay for it. But look, Styles. There's no blood on my hands." He held them out for me to see, smiling and smiling. Then he turned to Martin. "Call in the cop from the hallway, Ben. Hopefully he'll take Mr. Styles to a nice, padded retreat somewhere."

It was a shrewd play. I could see a totally frustrating future ahead of us. We didn't have proof. I hadn't the slightest doubt that I'd faced Capra with the truth, and very little hope that I could ever make it stick. He was too rich, had too much power, control over large segments of the media. There would be people who'd believe what I believed, but that wouldn't be enough to get him into court. Without solid evidence, I was whistling into the wind.

Ben Martin looked a little stunned, I thought, but he walked slowly to the front door. He paused there, turning back to Capra.

"You're sure, Stanley?"

"If Mr. Styles were to disappear, his friends would come here looking for him," Capra said. "They know he was aimed here. There's a policeman who came with him on the other side of that door. With some regret, I'm sure the sensible thing is to turn him loose."

Martin opened the front door and called out into the hall, "Okay, officer. Mr. Styles is ready to go."

I had a flash out of someplace in that moment. If I walked out that door with Zabriskie the ballgame was over. *It was what Capra wanted me to do so I must not do it!* There was Thelma Reeves's whispered plea for help. She had evidence, must be a witness to at least one crime. She was upstairs, packed, ready to be shipped or taken away to where we could never reach her. She was too terrified to speak while she was surrounded by Capra and Martin and Bond and God knows how many others in and around the building. Leave her in their hands and our only chance was gone.

Zabriskie appeared in the open doorway. He stood there, looking vague.

"Bon voyage, Mr. Styles," Capra said.

I didn't move from my place on the love seat. "I haven't finished my conversation with Miss Reeves," I said.

"Oh, I'm very much afraid you have," Capra said. That frozen smile was still there.

"Miss Reeves is up on the second floor," I said to Zabriskie. "I'd appreciate it if you'd bring her down."

Martin made a quick move to place himself between Zabriskie and the stairway.

"Are you going to threaten a police officer with a gun, Martin?" I asked. I looked at Capra. "It's a kind of stalemate, Capra. You pointed out yourself that people know I came here. Patrolman Zabriskie isn't the only one. There is a man watching every move you've made for the last twenty-four hours. If anything happens to me, he knows you're a witness. If I walk out of here, as you want, you're in the clear. If you try to get rid of me another way, you will have to do it with Patrolman Zabriskie as a witness. If you try to do away with him, you'll be in a nasty box. Cops don't like cop killers. I want to finish talking with Miss Reeves."

I could almost feel him balancing his choices.

"Ask Thelma to come down," he said to Martin.

Martin only went up a step or two and called. "Thelma! Stanley wants you down here."

She appeared after a moment. She had changed into a beige linen traveling suit. She was wearing a little hat with a veil that came down to the bridge of her nose.

"Mr. Styles thinks he has something more to discuss with you, my dear," Capra said. He turned to Martin. "Find out what's keeping Curtis."

Thelma Reeves came down the last steps into the room. The veil hid her eyes, making it impossible for me to guess what she was thinking.

"Is there any reason, Miss Reeves, why you and I can't go away from here for a private talk?" I asked her.

She glanced at Capra. "I have nothing to talk about," she said.

I could have reminded her that she'd asked me for help, but if I fumbled the ball in this game that could be a death warrant for her.

"You're about to travel somewhere," I said.

"Stanley's taking me abroad with him," she said.

"And you're delaying our departure," Capra said. "Now, Miss Reeves has made it quite clear, in front of this policeman, that she doesn't want to talk to you. We have rights, you know, Styles. You're invading our castle. Man's home, you remember? I think Patrolman Zabriskie must know that Miss Reeves has the legal right to ask you to leave. Tell him, my dear."

"Please, go," Thelma Reeves said. I think I've never heard such flat despair in a human voice. She had her choice to make, too. She didn't see me as any kind of match for Capra.

"The man's right, Mr. Styles," Zabriskie said. He went to the front door and opened it. He stood to one side, I thought at first to let me out. I didn't really believe what happened next. Suddenly, standing in the doorway, was Joe Steiger, a white mountain in his linen suit. Just behind him, erect, hard-faced, was Marilyn Travers.

"You okay, chum?" Steiger asked me, cheerfully.

I nodded.

He looked at Capra who was standing like a statue by the armchair. "The lady here had a gun she was going to use to kill you, Capra," he said, "but I took it away from her. She's been trying so hard to get to you I thought she ought to have a chance to speak her piece. We waited outside till we were sure Peter wasn't hanging by his fingernails somewhere. I guessed you'd send him away, sooner or later. Only smart thing for you to do."

Marilyn walked past Steiger and straight up to Capra. "You killed him!" she said. "I missed this time, Stanley, but sometime soon I won't miss. Maybe it's better this way. It will give you a chance to dream about it, to anticipate it."

I reached out and grabbed Thelma Reeves by the wrist. "This is your chance," I said. "It may be the only chance you'll ever have." I pulled her toward the door.

A gun shot shattered the quiet of the room. I looked back. Steiger, a gun in his hand, spoke to Ben Martin, who was down on his knees hugging a wounded arm.

"That was real foolish, friend, real foolish," Steiger said. "If the lady wants to go, you should let her go."

Thelma Reeves and I didn't hear anymore. We were clattering down the stairs, out onto the street, into the real world. The lady had decided to take her chances with me.

It took me about five running steps from the apartment entrance to Thelma's building, dragging the lady behind me, to realize that there was no miracle involved in our escape. Joe Steiger and Marilyn Travers had seemed like a miracle, but now we were surrounded by a small army of plainclothes cops. Among them, shaved and looking like a Madison Avenue ad man, was Sergeant Pat Cooper, my bodyguard from the night before.

"This Miss Reeves?" Cooper asked me.

"Miss Reeves, Sergeant Cooper," I said.

Thelma Reeves was hanging onto me as though she was about to go down for the third time. I patted one of her white knuckled hands. One of the cops was already holding open the door of a black limousine.

"The lieutenant wants you brought to his office," Cooper said.

"Maxvil?"

Cooper grinned at me. "His stakeout," he said.

Thelma and I sat in the back of the limousine. Cooper rode up front with the driver. Other cops followed us in a second car. Thelma lifted the little veil that covered her eyes and looked up at me.

"Ben Martin tried to shoot me!" she said.

"You just may have all the answers. Last ditch for them."

"The man in the white suit—the woman?" she asked.

"Joe Steiger is a private eye working for me. The woman is the widow of J. W. Travers," I said.

"Oh my God," she said. "How did they get there?"

"We're about to find out," I said. "The man we're on the way to see is my closest friend, Lieutenant Maxvil of Manhattan Homicide."

She leaned her head against my shoulder. "I—I thought you were going to leave me there," she said.

"You had to make the choice," I said.

The corridors and offices at police headquarters had always seemed bleak and hostile to me. That afternoon they felt wonderfully homelike and secure. I realized that I was haunted by the power, the far-reaching power, of Loring Industries. This was one place, I assured myself, they couldn't penetrate.

Maxvil, looking rather pleased with himself, rose from his desk as we were brought in.

"You are all right, Miss Reeves?" he asked.

She nodded. "Thanks to Mr. Styles," she said.

"Zabriskie has reported in," the lieutenant said to me. "They were just going to let you walk away, Peter?"

"I didn't have anything on them," I said. "But Miss Reeves had let me know she wanted help. I was trying to figure out how, when suddenly Joe Steiger was there—and Marilyn Travers."

"Sit down, Miss Reeves," Maxvil said. "Things opened

up rather suddenly." He sat down behind his desk and lit a cigarette. "Double stakeout. I had men there, and there was Steiger; Zabriskie didn't go into the apartment with you because he wanted to contact me—let me know you were inside with them. You see, I knew Capra and his pals were in the apartment. So did Steiger, who'd picked up Mrs. Travers. Everybody finally headed your way, Miss Reeves. Let me explain your situation to you."

"A choice of ways to die?" she suggested bitterly. "Stanley Capra or the state? I decided I preferred the state."

"You're not going to die, Miss Reeves," Maxvil said. "You're going to tell us what you know in return for your freedom, immunity from prosecution."

"What good is freedom, with Stanley's people waiting for me to stick my nose outside the door somewhere?"

"They're going to be too busy trying to save their own necks to bother with you," Maxvil said. "Where does it begin, Miss Reeves? With Rex Callison?"

"I killed him," she said.

Maxvil sat very still, his cold eyes fixed on her. "You mean you were responsible for his being killed?"

"Poor darling," she said. "I'd given him a very bad time, treated him like dirt, but he was willing to help. There was no one else I could turn to."

"Take your time, Miss Reeves. We have all day, all night, all next week to wrap up this package."

I'd had it right from the moment I'd first connected Rex Callison with the case. Thelma went back to before that night of November eighth. It was important to her that we understood about her relationship with Capra. Loring Industries, she explained to us, was, indirectly through one of its companies, one of the sponsors of "Secret Corridors," her television soap. It was Rubicon, the real estate people. Rubicon gave a party one night for the producers, the cast, the technicians of "Secret Corridors." Capra was at that party. The leading lady attracted him.

"He invited me to go somewhere with him when the party broke up," she told us. "He's attractive—till you know him well. He was, maybe, the richest man in the world. I—I thought it would be fun. Can you imagine champagne on the deck of a yacht, moonlight? Sex has been a matter of fun and games with me ever since I was sixteen. Not romance, just fun. Why not with Stanley Capra—who owned half the world—on a yacht, in the moonlight? I didn't owe any loyalty to anyone, not even Rex, who'd been a more-or-less steady sex partner for some years. It was understood that if I wanted to try something else I could, and if he wanted to try something else he could."

Stanley Capra wasn't interested in giving her up, once he'd gone past the first barrier. He offered her financial security she'd never dreamed of having, luxury she'd never imagined enjoying: clothes, jewels, anything on earth she wanted. The only condition was that she must give up her career, be available to him at any hour of any day, or night, or week, or month he wanted.

"He took me up the mountain, showed me the world, and I was dazzled," she said. Obviously the memory of it was painful now.

She told us that she found she was suddenly a prisoner, a slave. She couldn't walk out, because in the early days of their being together, Capra had boasted about what a big shot he was, amused her with stories of how he had smashed other powerful men. The world of dirty tricks. When she finally went to him and told him she didn't want to go on with this life any longer, he made it clear that she couldn't go. She knew too much about him. She could stay, let herself be used any way he wanted, or she would have to simply disappear. She knew from his boasting that staging a disappearance would be child's play for him. Now she was living in a climate of terror. She sometimes didn't see him for weeks when he was on the other side of the world somewhere. She never knew for sure where he was until she heard his key in the front door lock. But she knew she was always watched—by Mariotti in the upper apartment, by men who patrolled the neighborhood, perhaps even by the women who worked in the Delight Shoppe.

Finally Capra had been absent for several weeks. Thelma felt she couldn't stand it any longer. She had to be able to get help, she had to be able to discuss her problems with someone. The only person she could think of who she could trust was her ex-boyfriend, Rex Callison. She called his message service and left her number.

"That was last November eighth?" Maxvil asked.

"Yes, yes," she said. "Rex called after his show that night, offered to come to see me. He came. Stanley had been absent for so long I was sure he was in Europe, somewhere. I told Rex the spot I was in. And then, while we were talking, I heard Stanley's key in the lock! God help me."

Capra had come in, not alone, but accompanied by Ben Martin and Curtis Bond.

"Rex blew his stack," Thelma told us. "He shouted accusations that were true, things I had told him. And then, a little white knight on a little white horse, he rushed at Stanley. And Stanley snatched a gun out of his pocket and shot him—oh God, Lieutenant—right between the eyes."

From there on we'd already guessed the truth about that night. Martin and Bond were, of course, there to help. One of them drove a car around to the basement entrance. The other two carried Callison to the basement, took down the locking bar, scouted the street, saw Madison Fry coming, missed putting the locking bar back in place. When Fry came in, they had to attack him.

"Do you know how they disposed of Callison's body?" Maxvil asked.

"No. I wasn't to be trusted anymore. But I know why Jefferson Fry was killed a few months later in Vickers Creek."

Maxvil just stared at her, his eyes narrowed against the smoke from his cigarette—the fourth since we'd begun talking.

"Jefferson Fry was involved with his cause—fighting nuclear power. Stanley was a primary target. Jefferson Fry was somewhere in the neighborhood that night, in contact with his brother. I think Jefferson had his brother watching for . . . whatever. That night Madison Fry saw Rex Callison come to call on me—saw him ring my doorbell, heard me release the lock. He saw Jefferson a little later and told him that 'the lady had a boyfriend.' He'd recognized Rex from some movies he'd made. That wasn't particularly important to Jefferson until Rex's disappearance became news. Jefferson knew that Rex had been in my apartment. He also knew that Stanley and the others had arrived while Rex was still there. Two and two. He went to Stanley in Vickers Creek and told him he'd tell that story to the police unless the nuclear project there was abandoned. That was Jefferson's deadly mistake." Thelma drew a deep breath. "J. W. Travers began to make noises. Stanley was very angry. One night he asked me if I saw now what my doublecrossing behavior had cost? Another life! 'You might just as well have pulled the trigger!' he told me."

Thelma didn't have much more to tell us, but it was enough to put an end to Capra and Martin and Bond on the charge of murder and collaboration in committing a murder. Someone in Vickers Creek must have talked out of turn, the talk had reached Virgil Hardesty. He, in turn had contacted J. W. J. W. had gone to talk to Carmen Fry, who must have known what Jefferson knew, and been too terrified of Capra's power to go to the police. She had children to protect. J. W. must have been persuasive. He knew too much. He had to die, and Hardesty had to die. It had been like chain lightening, one flash after another.

None of the cases are closed now. The police and the FBI are back at it. The generals may be in jail, but there are foot soldiers to be caught. Thelma Reeves will testify. Carmen Fry, Maxvil thinks, can be persuaded to talk. Loring Industries, with new men in charge, will have to keep its nose clean for years to come.

And I? I walked out of Maxvil's office in the early evening and went to a telephone.

"I can buy you dinner tonight with nothing else on my mind but you," I told Beth Ryan.

"I'd love that," she said, "except that I'm not hungry for food."

"Whatever you are hungry for I'll be at your place in twenty minutes," I said.

And I was.